BRET NELSON

Encyclopocalypse Publications
www.encyclopocalypse.com

ISBN: 978-1-960721-29-7

Cover Design by Grim Poppy Designs
Cover Layout by Sean Duregger
Interior design and formatting by Sean Duregger
Edited by 360 Editing (a division of Uncomfortably Dark), Editor: Candace Nola

Foreword

From 1961 to 1976, World Cinema Group fed the drive-in and dollar theater markets with a mix of low-budget monster flicks and exploitation films. Over the course of those 15 years, they released over 40 features, mostly based on pulp magazine stories and sci-fi novellas of the day.

The single owner and engine behind WCG was Harold J. Kerr (1917-1983).

His parents ran a linen supply house for restaurants, and though successful (one of their clients was Howard Johnson's), the business held no interest for Harold. Instead, he worked for his uncle, Leonard Kerr, who owned six movie theaters in the Midwest. Harold ran promotions for the chain.

Like all theaters, the chain struggled to compete with television in the 1950s. At the end of that decade, Harold J. Kerr moved to Hollywood, intent on "creating the product rather than projecting it." With some seed money from his parents and a guaranteed run at his uncle's theaters, Kerr produced his first feature using his apartment on Cherokee Avenue as an office.

Doctor Shock's Carnival (1961) featured a lot of

stock footage of tilt-a-whirls and a completely over-the-top performance by Vincent Barbi as the titular villain. Kerr found distribution beyond his uncle's screens. This picture ran in nine states. It made a profit, thanks mainly to the outrageous poster and a title song by the then-popular rock band "The Pepper Grinders."

And for the next fifteen years, one picture paid for the next.

WCG "shaky" logo circa 1961

WCG "study" logo circa 1972

Most of these films are lost, as Kerr had strong opinions about distribution.

He'd seen his uncle trade movies on the sly with other theaters, dodging rental fees. It made Kerr obsessive about keeping track of his films. He struck very few prints and moved them from venue to venue on tight schedules with tight books.

Each time a print ran at a new theater, it eroded a bit more. When there were too many scratches or gaps, what was left of the print was returned to World

Cinema Group's offices on Gower Street in Hollywood. Kerr kept a hibachi in the alley behind the building where he burned the spent reels.

Rather than run off new prints of existing titles, Kerr often recut his older pictures to make "new" ones that he could send around the wheel again as a "fresh" movie.

Harold J. Kerr circa 1978

He never sold a film for television distribution. When asked about it, Harold J. Kerr, the man behind *Chain Whipping Biker Girls (1965)* and *Cannibal Hoedown (1970)*, said, "there's no value in the exploitive medium that is television."

This lack of TV distribution is why the WCG library is lost.

When he passed away in 1983, the remaining masters of his films were discovered. They'd been in a room at his Topanga Canyon home for decades. None were stored properly. Most of the reels were out of their cans, everything in teetering stacks. Ruined.

Today, this small Hollywood company's output exists only in the memories of the people who made the pictures and the people who saw them in theaters. Many will argue over which group is larger.

So, here are the beginnings of an archive. Kerr didn't believe television was a good idea, but he loved print. Many WCG pictures were adapted from pulp stories or dime novellas. Original WCG pictures *became* pulp stories or dime novellas after their theatrical runs.

The films may be lost, but the stories are not. Neither are the memories of the people who worked on them. In some cases, fragments of the production remain. And we are gathering them.

This is the first of a series collecting the tales that were World Cinema Group features. Harold J. Kerr said, "I don't expect any of my movies to make history. But I would like them to be like an eclipse...you only see it for a little while, but you remember it."

We do, Harold. We do.

Mark Alan Miller (July, 2023)
Owner, Encyclopocalypse Publications

For Colleen

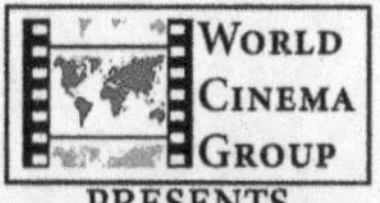

MURDER GARDEN

The edges of Theodore Raddison's eyes were a mix of yellows and reds.

They itched.

He pulled the tangle of blankets tighter around his shoulders and adjusted the cardboard under his hip. He'd arrived in the North London suburb of Dorling yesterday, and already collected four sacks of bottles. Later today they would be turned in for a bit of cash at the off-license.

This building had been vacant for ages, but it used to be a tailors. Raddison remembered the location from the last time he was in Dorling, three years ago. Or was it…he couldn't sort his memories anymore.

No, he was right, three years. It was 1970, the start of a brand-new decade.

Back then, he got inside the place through a window off the alley. Tonight, he found all the windows and doors boarded up tight. But Raddison didn't have anywhere else to go, so he huddled up against a wall and hoped no one would chase him away.

He'd slept a bit, but the sun had just crept over the hill. The occasional car passed.

Daytime. Noise and moving air.

Rest would come in fits now if it came at all. Soon, he'd need to find some booze.

Another car came down the road, but this one stopped and parked. He closed his eyes tight and pretended to sleep. The door opened; he sensed the driver approaching. Squinting, he felt relief when he saw it wasn't a copper.

"Oh, 'ello, squire," said Raddison. "Can you help a fella out?"

The driver moved closer and pressed a sweet-smelling cloth to Raddison's face. He plunged into sleep.

———

The Dorling Criminal Investigation Division's briefing room held a dozen restless officers. They wanted to clear their lists, rather than listen to Detective Chief Inspector Roger Weeks.

It was his fourteenth year at Dorling CID. He stood taller than most people, and though he ate constantly, he remained thin enough to worry his sister every time she saw him. In his early days on patrol, his slender appearance held him back, as his superiors didn't think he looked threatening enough to prevent street crime. One of his Sergeants kept putting his name on the rolls as "Weaks."

But Weeks had a secret weapon at his disposal, his voice.

When needed, Weeks' booming baritone made people listen. When he yelled "Hold it," they did. Thieves, running away with armloads of swag, froze and dropped the goods just because he told them to.

Now, that voice called a dozen officers to order.

"Right," said Weeks. "Settle in and we'll try to make this quick. We had another rough sleeper walk in a few hours ago. Said he witnessed a kidnapping. It sounds like the others; a big car stops and a tramp gets pulled off the street. The man who reported it says he wants something done before the same thing happens to him."

"Come on," said DI Michael Buchannon. "It's a bunch of meths drinkers passing around a scary story. They see goblins, pink elephants, and now, kidnappers." Buchannon had a year and a half until retirement age, and his only real interest was reaching sixty without injury or incident. He and his wife had already found a lovely place in Southport.

"These types don't come to police stations voluntarily," said Weeks. "This is the fifth time in a month we've had them up to the front desk. All different people reporting. It bears watching."

"Here's a bet," said Buchannon. "I'll lay you three-to-one each of these missing people got up to something shady. Had to sneak out-of-town, all quiet-like."

"I'm just asking for awareness, Mike," said Weeks, "So, everyone be aware there may be something worse than usual going on with this group. Another thing to be aware of; the royal wedding is just a few days away and as you know, we're all invited."

A groan moved around the room. "I may not be able to attend," said Constable Bennett. He had hoped for the day off so he could watch the wedding with his girl.

"Everyone is working," said Weeks. "They're calling in officers from all over. They need help with crowd control, punks grabbing cameras, that sort of thing. You're either working here or at Westminster. If you've been assigned to one but you'd like the other, find someone to swap with and bring the paperwork to me."

Weeks took a sip of his tea, then continued. "As you know, Princess Anne's nuptials will be the first royal wedding broadcast on television, in colour, around the world. So, all of you, watch what you're scratching."

Buchannon swept his bald head and spoke in a high voice. "I'll need a new frock if I'm going to be on telly." Laughter broke out all around.

"Quiet," said Weeks. "The plan is to gather up here and take vans into London. Times and specific duties will be on the board this afternoon. Talk to Constable Pixley at the front desk if you have questions."

He heard muttering. No one liked Constable Maurice Pixley. The fresh recruit was young and full of energy. Always asking questions. The higher-ups called him "a real go-getter."

The officers at Dorling CID called him "Pricksley."

"That's all I've got," said Weeks. "Anyone have anything to add?"

Silence.

"Then let's go," he said. "Watch yourselves." As the room emptied, Weeks motioned for Buchannon to join him at the tea cart. "Mike, a moment."

"Sorry, boss. Just keeping it light, you know."

"It's not that, Mike. Can't wait to see your new frock, by the way. I've got a call this morning with the Superintendent. What can I tell her about this car theft ring?"

"It's a long operation. Our undercover man is working at one of the repair shops we know is involved. He's expecting a breakthrough this week. I've got a call scheduled with him tonight."

Weeks stared into his tea, forming the words he'd use with his boss. "So, he's putting a picture together, making progress."

"Exactly right," said Buchannon. "He *has* confirmed Dexter Barnes and his crew are behind the thing."

"He's certain? Barnes has criminal enterprises running from here to Birmingham, but we can't make anything stick."

"That's why our man, Pierce, is taking his time finding solid evidence. So far, he's been dealing with old Walt Lymon. We all know *that* savage bastard."

"Yeah, he's been Dexter's muscle going way back.

You're right, if old Walt is in this, Barnes is in it as well. Thanks, Mike."

As the two stepped toward the door, Constable Pixley trotted in. "Good morning," he said. "Thought you'd like to know, there's a nude couple in the cells. Married, in their fifties. Separate rooms, of course, Sir."

Buchannon never broke his stride. Stepping out the door, he called back to Weeks. "Good luck with it."

"Why does this keep happening?" asked Weeks.

"Don't know, Sir," said Pixley. "But it's not just here. Similar cases are popping up all over."

———

Gravel crunched under the wheels of Walt Lymon's blue Vauxhall as he drove around the back of Dorling Tyre and Auto Repair. His boss, Dexter Barnes, owned the place.

The shop's manager, Nick Sanders, had a clear view of the alley behind the shop from the window of his upstairs office. He watched Lymon waiting in his car.

"Maybe he'll stay there," muttered Sanders. These visits made him uneasy.

After a few minutes, a van from Gladdom's Blooms joined Walt in the alley. Gladdom's had flower shops all over, but their delivery vehicles were serviced right here. Sanders wondered what business they had with Walt, but he quickly put it out of his mind and returned to his work.

Sanders had been running this shop for twenty-seven years now, the last five of them for Dexter Barnes. They had a lot of break-ins five years ago and the police were no help. Once Barnes came on as a partner, the robberies stopped. Extra jobs came in as well, some of them shady, but Sanders didn't mind.

He heard the engines start in the alley and saw the van drive away. He hoped to see Walt follow them, but instead, the Vauxhall came around and parked in the front.

"Bugger," said Sanders.

Walt Lymon came through the roll up doors with loud greetings and forced laughter. The rumples in his blue suit and his darting eyes meant he'd been up all night, fueled by booze and crank.

"Hello, all! How are we this morning?" asked Walt. A chorus of good wishes came from all around the shop, but Walt didn't hear them over his coughing fit.

Upstairs at the end of the shop, Nick Sanders popped out of his office. "Hello, sir!" he said. "Do you need me?"

"No, I'm fine on my own. I won't be long. Quick stop here, then home to bed."

"All right, then," said Sanders. "I'll be close if anything comes up. Where's Nigel?"

Nigel Wilkes was Walt's right hand, a schemer no one trusted.

"I've got decades on the kid, and he can't keep up with me," said Walt. "He's asleep in the car."

"You're a marvel," said Sanders. He retreated to the office, and the rest of the crew returned to their work, hoping Walt hadn't come for them.

"Jerry?" called Walt. "Is Jerry Gordon here?"

"Yessir?" The voice came from underneath a Ford Cortina. Jerry Gordon rolled out on a creeper.

"I keep telling you, call me Walt."

"Sorry, old habits, you know?" He stood, tucked the spanner into his back pocket, and wiped his hands on a rag.

"Sadly yes, I do know," said Walt. "Everyone is 'Sir,' or you lose a privilege, eh? Tell me again, how long was you away in Brixton?"

Jerry Gordon grew a short beard as soon as he got out. Jet black, just like his wavy hair. "Six months," he said. "Good behavior and overcrowding got me out early. Not planning on going back, either."

"No one ever 'plans' on going back," said Walt. He chuckled at himself and had another coughing fit. Gordon marveled at the twists and scars on Walt's knuckles and fingers as he covered his mouth with enormous, knobby hands.

"Well," said Gordon, "as long as I keep away from trouble—"

"Bollocks," said Walt. "I know plenty of people who got tossed back in the clink, even though they did nothing. No matter how clean you're keeping your nose, the coppers will come for you just because you've got form."

"They can do that?" Jerry Gordon knew full well they could do that. In fact, he had done it himself. His real name was Graham Pierce. His actual hair colour was blonde, and he used to be clean shaven, but right now he was working undercover for Dorling CID.

"They're coppers. They can do anything they like," said Walt. He spat, then continued. "You wait and see. They'll have a robbery or some such thing on the books and you'll get brung in to help with their inquiries. If you don't have an alibi, you're cooked. Back to Brixton you go just because your history lines up with the crime. Wankers."

"I'll make sure I always have an alibi, then. What can I do for you, Walt?"

Walt rubbed his nose and sniffed. "There's some after-hours work coming in. How would you like some extra money?"

"What sort of work?"

Walt's eyes narrowed. "It's on cars."

"Sorry," said Gordon. "Didn't mean anything by it."

"No harm, son," said Walt. "I know you're worried about ending up back in the jug. But this isn't stealing or rigging up brakes. All you'll do is move those tools about for an extra bit of pocket money."

"Sounds good."

"Smart lad." Walt gave him a friendly slap on the cheek. "Not sure exactly which, but it will be a night this week." He called to the office. "Oi! Sanders!"

He reappeared at the top of the stairs. "Yes, Walt?"

"The frame is out in the world, so night work's coming in. Got you another set of hands for it. Young Mr. Gordon. What do you think?"

"Sounds fantastic. He's much better than the last sod you brought in here, name of Clyde. In his cups, on arrival. Kept dropping things. Useless, like a paper teapot."

"He was me brother-in-law."

Sanders grew pale. "Blimey. Sorry, Walt."

"No offence taken, Sanders. He is a right pointless individual. It's why we had to let him go. I don't think you'll be seeing him for a while."

"Why?" asked Gordon.

"He's serving at Her Majesty's pleasure in Dartmoor. Got in a bar fight and knifed a Cabinet Minister's son."

Nigel Wilkes, looking puffy and worn past his twenty-five years, stumbled in, and stood next to Walt. "Hello all," he said, as if in charge. "Is there tea?"

"No," said Walt. "We're leaving. And you're driving."

II

The warmth from the fire loosened the joints in Theodore Raddison's hands. He rolled them into a pair of fists, then stretched his fingers straight. No popping, no pain.

Looking past his hands, he wondered where he was. He often found himself in unfamiliar surroundings. Once, he took a sip from a bottle in Hyde Park, then he snapped awake at a train station in Montpellier. He was in the middle of a conversation with a policeman.

Now, he sat in a soft wingback chair. Nearby, wood paneling and books around a fireplace. This wasn't a pub, no tables. But it was posh. *Don't react,* he thought. *If you're supposed to be here and you jump, they might kick you out.* A few feet away he saw another chair, identical to his, facing the fire. Its occupant reviewed papers on a clipboard.

A man in his forties. Tight brown hair and a goatee. He wore jeans, and his dark grey jumper had a shirt collar peeking out from the top. His trainers were new, looked expensive. These clothes spoke of home, not work.

The man's eyes lifted from his papers to Raddison. "Ah, you are with us," he said.

"Yes," said Raddison, feeling his way.

"Need your name."

"Pardon?"

"Your name," the man said. He took a pen from the top of the clipboard and tapped it on the papers. "For this form, I need your name, please."

"Oh, of course. Theodore Raddison. Raddison has two D's in the middle, like 'middle.'"

The man smiled as he wrote. "Clever. Age?"

"Sixty-two. Say, what's this for?"

"It is for accuracy, Mr. Raddison."

"Not sure I got your name, friend."

"It is Marchworth. Doctor Fredrick Marchworth." The doctor stood and snapped the clipboard under his arm. "Wrist, please."

"Pardon?"

Marchworth lifted Raddison's arm and pressed two fingers to his wrist. "Noting your pulse, Mr. Raddison."

"What's this all about?" asked Raddison.

"Quiet, please," said Marchworth, counting in his head. Raddison buttoned his lip, but his unease grew. How long had he been here? And these clothes were new. Not his.

He remembered the street and the car rolling up. The doctor released his wrist and made another note on his form. "Pulse is surprisingly strong," he said.

"Hang on a tick," said Raddison. "I appreciate your hospitality and your…concern. But I'm a little hazy. Where am I?"

"You are in my care," said Marchworth. "Your belongings—the blankets, the bottles, the clothes—are all safe and stored."

"I don't understand. Say, is there any whiskey about?"

"Sorry," said Marchworth. He walked behind Raddison's chair and appeared on the other side. "It will interfere with your fluids." He motioned to a pair of IV bottles hanging from a stand and tapped one of them with his pen.

Raddison hadn't looked over there. The tube from the IV bottle led behind him. He felt along its length to a catheter in his head. "Here, what is this?"

Past the IV stand, the rest of the room was vast, and quite different from the paneled study area where he sat. The floor and walls transitioned to white tile. Bright lights, electronic equipment, and medical gear were packed around a large hospital bed.

Marchworth moved Raddison's hand away from the tubing. "Please, do not touch that," he said. "You may cause yourself harm."

"Harm? Blimey, who are you?" Raddison shifted in his chair. "Hey, why can't I get up?"

"Because your legs have been injected with a paralytic. The effect is temporary. Please, calm down."

Raddison leaned forward and back. Struggled to move. "Calm down? You mad bastard, let me go!"

With a sigh, Marchworth twisted a valve on the IV and Raddison went limp. The doctor checked the pulse again.

"Yes, quite strong," he said. "You get some more rest, Mr. Raddison. We have a lot of work to do. And I need you to survive."

———

DI Mike Buchannon tapped on DCI Weeks' door.

Weeks called from his desk, "Come." Buchannon entered with files under his arm. Weeks hung up the phone and sighed.

"What was that?" asked Buchannon.

"Anthony, my brother," said Weeks. "The one who works at Station Hospital. Go ahead, sit down."

Buchannon plopped into a chair. "Good news?"

"Hardly. Mrs. Weaver's in again. She's a mess."

Buchannan's face soured. "The old man at her again?"

"Seventy years old," said Weeks. "She's got concussion, and she took a bus to the hospital. Can you imagine? Scarf around her face to cover the marks."

"We should go have a word with Mr. Weaver."

"What's the use? She never presses charges. Never leaves. No kids to help her out and his pension is all she's got."

"She's got a lot of excuses, as well," said Buchannan. "She fell on the stairs. She bumped into a door. She got scraped up gardening."

"Yeah," said Weeks. "With so much stumbling around, you'd think *she* was the boozer." He stared into his tea. "Anthony says she was in a state, muttering disconnected things. They gave her something to help her sleep, but the bit pulling at me is she kept saying the old man wasn't moving."

"I'd guess it happens a lot with him drinking himself legless all day," said Buchannon. "Still, maybe we should send uniform around. Is Bennett on?"

"Why Bennett?" asked Weeks.

"Because he's not Constable Pricksley. And he knows the situation over there. He can handle the old man."

"I'll send him over. What did you need?"

Buchannon pulled out his notebook. "Just got a radio call about a car frame. The Traffic Division is on their way to pick it up. It's on Pearview Road. Full car frame, sitting just off the tarmac."

"Bet it's from one we've got missing. Pierce should be notified."

"I'll tell him on our call tonight." said Buchannon. "You know, there's not many who could have got it there. You'd need a flatbed with a winch and all."

"Who do we know with the gear for this kind of thing?"

"I know one for certain. Trillian, Johnny Trillian." Buchannon tossed a file onto Weeks' desk. "Working for his brother at Trillian's Towing and Recovery. He's got form."

Weeks flipped through the file. The twenty-three-year-old had a long record of burglary and auto theft. "Is he part of Barnes' crew?"

"Maybe. Let's invite him to help us with our inquiries, then we can ask."

———

The payphone mouthpiece smelled of garlic. Still, Nigel Wilkes had to make his afternoon calls. Between his cigarette, the coins he thumbed into the slot, the bits of paper with the numbers on them, and the handset, he barely managed.

"If the buyer can be specific about what they're after, I'll do my best to find it next time we see the doctor," he said. "Don't know when that will be, though. We were at his place on Boulton Heath early this morning, dropped one off and collected one for the garden. …Yes, I nicked those papers from the bin. It's just as we thought. Once he copies his notes all tidy, he chucks the rough versions. Ours for the taking. … No, I can't make head or tail of it. But if the buyer wants them, the papers are in hand. …Right, cheers, Mate."

He took a moment to steel himself, then dialed the last call on his list. He hoped Walt wasn't still sleeping.

The other end of the line clicked. "Hello?"

Relief. Walt sounded alert.

"It's me," said Nigel. "Vauxhall's washed with a full tank, like you wanted."

"The tyres?"

"Yes, they did the treatment on the tyres. All shiny."

"Bloody marvelous," said Walt. "Bring it round in an hour or so, then we'll head out."

"There are a couple of things you should know.

The fuzz picked up that frame. Should be calling the owner in the next day or so once they've looked it over." He heard Walt's lighter sparking, followed by a coughing fit.

"Terrific," said Walt, choking. "What else?"

"I got a call from Trillian's. Johnny's been pinched."

Silence.

Nigel continued. "Just as he left work. He got past the gate and they put him in a car."

Nigel heard Walt draw deep on his cigarette. "Cuffs?"

"I asked. No cuffs. I talked to our friend in blue and he said Johnny was brung in to 'help with their inquiries.' Likely won't be held."

"Keep talking to our friend in blue," said Walt. "I want to know when Johnny gets out. Any word from Boulton Heath? Does the Professor need anything?"

"I called but got no answer. Working, most likely, you know how he does. But it means he's probably happy with the goods."

III

Late in the afternoon, Jerry Gordon clocked out at Dorling Tyre and Auto Repair. On the long drive to his flat in the neighbouring town of Serkin, he became DS Graham Pierce again. He parked in front of his building and walked across the street to the newsagent's.

"Hello Detective Pierce. The rain has stopped, yes?"

"Good to see you, Mr. Hamadi, Mrs. Hamadi," said Pierce. "It has stopped, yes. Nice out now." He tucked a copy of the Times under his arm and began arranging coins on the counter.

"Here's for the paper," he said. "And let's have a bag of those red Hula Hoops, and another bag as well, and a four-pack of White Shield, please."

Emran Hamadi deftly placed the items into a right-sized bag as his wife punched numbers into the till. She kept looking at her husband, growing cross. "Aren't you going to ask him, Emran?"

"Stop Nadia. Detective Pierce is just on his way home. He's not working."

"He can answer a question. I'm sure he wouldn't mind," said Mrs. Hamadi. "You wouldn't mind, would you, Detective Pierce?"

Pierce became curious. "Ask me anything you like," he said.

Mr. Hamadi took a deep breath. "They said we weren't to speak to the police. But at this moment, you are simply my customer, right?"

"Who said you weren't to speak to the police?" Pierce put his shopping back on the counter, anticipating this might take some time.

"It's these young men," said Mr. Hamadi. "They live over in Wilbur Estates."

"I know the Estates. What did these young men do to you?"

"Nothing, as yet. But they said they'd be in next week. They said they were coming in with some merchandise and we were to put it on the shelf."

"What sort of merchandise?"

"Crisps, if you can believe it," said Mr. Hamadi. "We've had some thugs try to make us take their illegal cigarettes before, but I don't know where or how you get unlicensed crisps."

"They told us they were our supplier now," said Mrs. Hamadi. "They said if we didn't agree, they would hurt Emran. And break windows. And if we call the police, they will do even worse."

"They probably got hold of stolen merchandise. Do you know their names?"

"I think one is called Terry," said Mr. Hamadi. "There were three of them, and that's the only name I heard."

Pierce handed Mrs. Hamadi a card. "I'll make some inquiries. If they come back, just agree to whatever they say, then call this number."

"But what if they want money?" she asked.

"Tell them you just made the bank run, so there's no cash."

"That may not be good enough," said Mr. Hamadi.

"It will have to be for now," said Pierce. "Without evidence a crime has been committed, there isn't much I can do."

"All right, I guess we'll have to wait and see," said Mr. Hamadi. "Have a nice evening."

"You too," said Pierce. The Hamadi's smiled as he left.

"I told you he can't do anything," said Mr. Hamadi. "The police are no good for things like this. Just like back home."

"You're right," said Mrs. Hamadi. "We should call those people who work for Mr. Barnes. We pay money for protection, and I think it's time we got some."

———

Jamie Palmer bounced off the wall and landed on the floor in front of Nigel. His broken nose poured blood. It made his breathing staggered and wet.

The blow could've been worse. Walt lost his balance as he swung, otherwise Jamie's head may have flown clean off. Instead, Walt spun and stumbled into a file case. The corner of it tore his jacket.

"Bugger," said Walt. "Brand new." His drunken speech was slurred. His drunken eyes squinted at the torn seam. His crank-fueled anger took him over the edge.

Nigel saw the fit coming. "Easy Walt." He tried to make Palmer see reason. "Jamie, where's the money?"

"I told you," he gasped, spitting out blood. "I made the bank run today, a deposit. I just gave you all the cash in the house. First thing tomorrow, as soon as the bank opens, you'll have the rest."

Walt tossed the file case over, then flipped the desk. It raised an awful racket, but no one heard. The only person in the record shop was Palmer, the owner. They had closed half an hour before.

"I think he's had enough," said Nigel.

Walt crossed the room on shaky legs and kicked Palmer's ribs. "He's had enough when we get what's owed. You've been light on the last three drops, Jamie. It's two hundred quid, all told."

"I didn't know you were coming tonight." Palmer had trouble getting the words out. "You're usually in on a Wednesday. Tomorrow…the bank… you can meet me there if you like. But if you put me in hospital, I can't get there."

"He's got a point," said Nigel. "I believe him. Besides, Johnny Trillian will be out by now. We need to find him.

———

Doctor Marchworth's narcotic regimen worked with the hypnotic blips and tones from the machines around the hospital bed to keep his subject on the edge of cognition.

"I feel odd," said Raddison.

Tangles of red and blue wire connected the monitoring equipment to leads taped to thirty-six different points on Raddison's body. There were three catheters in his head now, instead of just one. Tubes branched out from the catheters, connecting to a series of filters and catch-vials. The system of tubes terminated with fourteen lines, each connected to a different, colour-coded syringe. The syringes sat in a row on an elevated tray next to the bed, some for extracting fluids, and others for pushing them in.

"Be still," said Marchworth, studying a strip of paper generated by one of his machines. "Nearly there."

With a careful eye on his readings, the doctor pulled on the third syringe and pushed in the tenth. Raddison's eyes went wide. "What's that?" he said.

"I am separating compounds from your brain," said Marchworth. "I shall use them to tune your mind and body."

Raddison explored the front of his gums with his tongue. "I'd like something sweet."

"Apple juice," said the doctor, pulling on the fifth syringe. "You want apple juice, and you will have some when this phase is finished."

"Yes," said Raddison, smiling. "Yes, just the thing."

"Your craving for apple juice is a good sign, Mr. Raddison. It means you are becoming."

"Becoming? Becoming what?"

"Becoming what is next," said Marchworth. "A new kind of human being. The part of your mind I am dealing with is called the 'behavioural central column.' Sounds like a prison ward, does it not?"

The doctor added a new syringe, much larger than the others, to the tray. "I have come to set you free."

X

Constable Bennett drove the patrol car through town on the way to the Weaver house. He'd been there a few weeks ago because Mr. Weaver, drunker than usual, got into a shouting match with a neighbour and it escalated to blows. No charges were filed.

This trip, he hoped to find Mr. Weaver passed out and quiet.

At a traffic light, movement in the rear-view mirror drew Bennett's attention. It took some time for him to process what he saw… a naked man.

He giggled and skipped with rhythm. Joyous.

Bennett stepped out of the car and pulled off his coat, holding it toward the nature lover. "Right, you," he said. "That's enough of that. Sir? Stop. Stop right now."

The man saw Bennett approaching and stopped skipping. A bright, enormous smile grew on his face, and he leapt to the officer with his arms outstretched, ready to give a hug.

Using his coat as a barrier, Bennett kept the man's nethers at bay. At the same time, he used the hug to hold the man in place. The officer's volley of questions and instructions were ignored. There wasn't any struggle, though. The bare citizen happily moved in concert with Bennett.

He was still ecstatic sitting on a blanket in the back of the car, with handcuffs on his wrists. Down the street, Bennett found the man's clothing, dropped piece by piece like breadcrumbs. His groceries and a bunch of flowers were strewn about the gutter. Bennett gathered up the clothes, but a passing bus destroyed the rest.

———

Once released, Johnny Trillian knew he'd be seeing Walt and Nigel. He'd have to explain what he said during his interview. He'd have to convince them he didn't embarrass Mr. Barnes.

He had said nothing to the police, but he'd probably get pretty bruised up before Walt believed him. So, Trillian didn't go home. Too easy to find him there. Instead, he wandered the streets, trying not to be seen.

He failed.

"Oi! Johnny!" Walt's voice thundered from across the street. As Nigel dodged cars to get to the other side, Johnny vanished into an alley.

"Johnny! Don't be a prat," called Walt. "We just want to talk."

The alley came to a dead end. Johnny spoke quickly as he looked for a way out. "There's nothing to talk about! I didn't say anything!"

Nigel entered the alley well ahead of Walt and found Trillian scrambling up a fire escape.

"For Chrissake, Johnny, are you an acrobat all the sudden?" shouted Nigel. "Get down from there."

Trillian climbed higher; eyes locked on Walt as he strutted into the alley. "I know to keep my lip buttoned," Trillian called, "and that's just what I done!"

Walt and Nigel shared a look, each hoping the other had a plan to get the man down. Nigel shrugged. Walt shook his head.

"It's fine, Johnny. Everything is all right," shouted Walt. "We just want to go over what happened is all.

Make sure we're telling it right when we talk to Dex."

"Listen to him," said Nigel. "Let's go have a pint. Sort this out."

"I don't believe you, and I don't want to get clobbered!" Johnny had nearly reached the roof. "Keep away!"

Then Johnny stepped toward a railing that wasn't there and dropped six floors to his death. The only witnesses were Walt and Nigel.

"Bugger," said Walt.

"What now?" asked Nigel.

"I'll stay here. You bring the car around. We'll take him to Gladdom's Blooms on Crestmore Street. He's going to the garden."

IV

Graham Pierce's flat smelled of last night's curry takeaway. He'd left in a hurry this morning, knocking his routine off center, so the kitchen bin didn't get emptied, and it stunk up the place. The post didn't get sorted either, and another batch sat on the floor in front of the slot.

First things first, he had to eat. He put his purchases from the newsagent's on the counter and checked the cupboard. There were two tins of good soup. A fine meal with some toast.

He got the soup in a pot. The cans topped off the foul kitchen bin, so he took out the rubbish and hurried back. On the way, he remembered he only had one clean shirt left.

Food first, he thought, *then maybe I can manage a run to the late-night launderette.*

Halfway through his meal, the phone rang.

"Bugger." He brought his soup to the desk. DI Buchannon was right on time for their briefing.

"So, what have we learned?" asked Buchannon.

"We've learned the repair shop is an actual business. It opens at eight and usually closes around four. But there's people in and out all night. Rough types."

"Good thing you know cars."

"Three generations," said Pierce.

"You had any dealings with Dexter Barnes?"

"Not yet. Spending more time with Walt Lymon and his toady, Nigel Wilkes. Oh, and a few days ago I met Pat Chandler."

"Well, this seals it," said Buchannon. "He's Barnes' most trusted lieutenant, so this all points at Dexter. What did you talk about?"

"I just got introduced. A handshake is all. He went straight into the office and left a few hours later."

"Damn," said Buchannon. "Pat Chandler is second in command, but from what I hear, he runs the day-to-day for Barnes. If you can get close to Chandler—"

"I know. It will come in time. They've got me on some shady after-hours thing later in the week. Something to do with a frame."

"Traffic found a pristine car frame on Pearview earlier today."

"That's got to be it. Got to be the one they mentioned. Still don't understand how this all works, though."

"Here's what I'll do...the frame will get pushed through the process. Tomorrow, we'll have it released to the owner, then track where it goes."

"Yes. I bet it goes to Dorling Tyre and Auto Repair," said Pierce. "We're getting close, I can feel it." He spotted the bag on his counter. "Hey, have you heard anything about a load of stolen crisps?"

"You'll have to say that again, Graham."

"My newsagent's said some young punks tried to force them into purchasing crisps in quantity. Must be swag, right?"

"Sounds like a lot of nothing, but I'll ask around," said Buchannon. "Gotta go. Let's talk again tomorrow night. You watch yourself."

"I will," said Pierce. "You be careful as well."

Buchannon hung up the phone and got ready to leave the station. As he passed the front desk, he found Bennett filling in forms.

"Sorry Sir," said Bennett. "Haven't been to the Weaver house yet. Ended up bringing in another nudie-looney."

———

The blue Vauxhall pulled in behind Gladdom's Blooms on Crestmore Street. One of their delivery vans sat parked near the loading area. There were people in the van. Walt and Nigel were expected.

Walt killed the engine and tossed the keys to Nigel. "Get it done," he said. Nigel hopped out the passenger side and did a half jog to the van. He got the attention of the driver, handed him a stack of cash, then trotted back to the Vauxhall and opened the boot.

He returned to the passenger seat, out of breath. He gave the keys back to Walt, who was busy forcing powder into his nose.

Two men from Gladdom's, barely silhouettes in the alley lights, took Johnny Trillian's body from the back of the car, closed the boot, and carried it to their van. Once they stowed it away, the driver flashed his headlights.

"Done and done," said Walt. "Switch with me. You should drive."

———

The Weaver home was tiny, but neat as a pin. Mrs. Weaver did her best to keep the place nice. They'd lived there for fifty years.

Buchannon parked at the rear and knocked on the back door. He'd opted to check on Pernell Weaver while Bennett processed his naked public nuisance.

No answer. "Drunken bastard," he said.

He knocked again. "Mr. Weaver? Are you home?"

The door wasn't locked, so Buchannon went in and spoke firmly. "Hello? This is the police. I'm Detective Inspector Michael Buchannon. Come to see if you are well, Mr. Weaver. Your wife is in hospital. Is anyone here?"

He made his way through the kitchen. An open whiskey bottle and a half-empty glass were on the table. Alongside those, a full ashtray, and the old man's cigarettes. Buchannon kept moving to the entrance hall. "Hello? Is anyone home?"

There, on the stairs leading up to the bedroom, Mr. Weaver's corpse lay on its back. His arms were at his sides, with his head on the lowest step and his feet pointing to the upper floor. No blood, but his neck was clearly broken.

Pernell Weaver was a mean old drunk and he should have died years ago, but these circumstances were difficult.

Weaver's forehead had a bump and broken pieces of a large vase were all around him. A small side table at the top of the stairs was the vase's former home. Bloody bits of cotton and a tube of Savlon were in the bathroom at the top of the stairs.

A picture formed in Buchannon's mind, showing him what had happened.

The old man beat on her, and she ran upstairs to see to her wounds. He sat at the kitchen table, getting drunker and nastier. Then he started in on her again. He probably shouted, coming up the stairs, and she tossed the vase.

She had concussion. Not in her right head. He goes down. She's scared and dizzy, so she goes to the bus, to the hospital.

Buchannon pulled out his notebook and looked at it for a long time. "Can't report this," he said, and tucked the notebook away.

He paced around, thinking out loud. "We'd have to arrest her. Even if it's self-defense, she'll lose the widow's portion of his pension." He walked through each room in the house three times, working out what he'd put in his report. Once he had the story sorted out, he used the kitchen phone to call Station Hospital.

"Hello, this is Detective Inspector Mike Buchannon with Dorling CID," he said. "May I speak to Doctor Weeks, please? Anthony Weeks…I see, can I leave a message then? Thank you, it's regarding a patient, Eudora Weaver. …I've done a check at her house; she's concerned about her husband. Well, he's fine. Found him sleeping, a bit intoxicated, I think, but well enough to give me a piece of his mind. That's the message, you have it? …No, it's a 'c-h' in Buchannon…thank you. Good night."

Buchannon had an old blanket in the back of his car, and he used it to roll up Weaver. The way to the car was clear, making it simple to get him from the house to the boot. The skinny old sod barely weighed more than the blanket.

Back inside, he made one more phone call. Then,

he grabbed the old man's hat off the hook and his cig-arettes off the kitchen table. He also plucked three butts from the ashtray and put them in his pocket.

After one more quick look-around, Buchannon locked up the house, then drove to Gladdom's Blooms on Crestmore Street.

———

"The beta waves are rising, Mr. Raddison," said Marchworth, eyeing one of his monitors. "Your habits have caused damage to the frontal area of your brain, but these numbers point to rapid healing." He scribbled some notes.

Theodore Raddison hadn't heard a word. He lay panting on the hospital bed with a pump shunting nutrition compounds into his digestive system. The three small catheters in his head had been replaced with a single large one.

"I can't see," said Raddison. "It hurts everywhere. Not just my eyes. Please, I need a doctor."

"I am a doctor!" said Marchworth. "How dare you! Most of the others failed to make it this far. You should be pleased."

Raddison wept.

———

DI Buchannon arrived at Treacher's Park. As he had hoped, it was deserted. He'd made an efficient drop-off at Gladdom's and if he got in and out of here without interruptions, he'd be home before the late news.

He gathered the items from the Weaver house and made his way to the walking path. He dropped the cigarette pack and the hat over the rail separating the path from the river, making sure they landed in the brambles at the edge, not in the water. Then, he dropped the three butts on the path by the rail.

"Farewell, you drunken old prat."

He stopped at the phone box by the gazebos on his way back to the car.

V

The next morning, Jerry Gordon arrived at Dorling Tyre and Auto Repair twenty minutes early. Nick Sanders, the manager, pulled one of the rolling doors up. "Cheers, Jerry. You can't clock in until eight, though."

"I know, I know. I got lucky today. All the traffic lights were in my favour."

"There's a fruit machine at The Ragged Lion. You should give it a few spins at lunch."

"I might at that."

Their discussion got interrupted by the screech of tyres. An older Riley tore down the road. "Noisy," said Sanders. "It's Nigel's Four-Sixty-Eight."

Nigel Wilkes roared across the gravel and parked. He was talking from the moment he opened the door. "Have you seen Walt? Has he called?"

"No one's called," said Sanders, "and I've not seen Walt since yesterday."

"Well, that's just great, that is," said Nigel. "You seen him, Jerry?"

"I only just got here," said Gordon.

Nigel paced a tight circle. "Pat's going to be here any minute," he said. "We're meant to help him out this morning. Walt didn't show up to collect me. No answer when I called."

"Doesn't sound like it's your fault," said Gordon. "Won't Pat understand?"

"It's Mr. Chandler to you," said Nigel. He turned to Sanders. "This is a two-man job. Let me take Gordon. It's only for a couple of hours."

Sanders shook his head. "I didn't cock this up. Why should I be a man down? Gordon's needed here." He motioned up the road to an approaching Aston Martin DBS. "And look what's coming."

Pat Chandler had arrived. He was a boxy man, tucked neatly into a tailored suit. Square shoulders, square head. Old as Walt, but Chandler had more life in him. He took quick steps to the men in front of the garage. "Hello all, are we well?" he said.

Greetings popped off all around.

"Nick," said Chandler, "the Aston runs beautifully now."

"Good to hear," said Sanders. "We need to get your carburettor cleaned out every couple of months, hard as you drive it."

"It made a big difference, thanks." Still smiling, Chandler locked his eyes on Nigel. "Where's bloody Walt?" he said. "I'm fifteen minutes late and he's still not here?"

"I'm sure he'll be along any minute," said Nigel.

"Don't cover for him. Bad form, that. Especially with me." Pat Chandler looked skyward for a moment, thinking.

He turned to Gordon. "You! What's your name again?"

"Jerry Gordon, Sir."

"Sir? You hear that, Nigel. You might learn a thing or two from him." Chandler reached into his pocket and brought out a roll of money. He counted off ten notes and handed them to Sanders. "I've got an errand. Need two people with me. I'd like to have young Gordon here on loan. Will this cover you if he's gone for a few hours?"

"It's exactly the right amount," said Sanders, smiling. "What are the odds?"

"Good." Chandler moved Nigel Wilkes and Jerry Gordon to the Riley.

"Are we taking my car?" asked Nigel.

"I'm not getting my Aston anywhere near Wilbur Estates." Chandler opened the car doors. "Nigel, you'll drive there. Jerry, you'll drive back. Get moving. I want this dealt with before my elevenses with Dex."

———

"Right," said DCI Roger Weeks. "Settle in and we'll try to make this quick."

The briefing room came to order. Weeks held up the latest issue of *The Sun.* The grainy photo on the front page showed an officer doing his best to shield a nude woman with his coat and helmet.

The headline read: *Tonight, on SPECIAL BRANCH, a cover up!*

The room exploded with laughter.

"Yeah, yeah. Calm down. We had another one of these last night. No one knows what's causing this. A fad? Some new drug? In all cases, the people claim to have no memory of the incident. It's something to watch for."

"Watch for?" said Bennett. "How could we miss it? I can't get this bloke from yesterday out of my head. All of him just wobbling. He was naked, but you couldn't see the naughty bits for the gut he had hanging."

Boos and catcalls. Weeks dropped into his baritone. "Moving on. No tramps have been reported missing in the last twenty-four hours, so whatever it is you're all doing, it's working. Keep at it."

He opened a folder and pulled out a photo. "You may have noticed DS Adams isn't here. He's investigating a missing person, presumed dead, last seen at Treacher's Park late last night."

As the room murmured, Weeks pinned the file photo on the board. "Pernell Weaver, age seventy-four."

"Blimey," said Bennett, "I was meant to see him."

"Yes, it's the same man," said Weeks. "Many of you have had run-ins with Mr. Weaver over the years. DI Buchannon ended up calling at the Weaver's home."

"I did," said Buchannon. "His wife was in hospital and concerned Mr. Weaver may have been unwell. As I wrote in my report, I checked in on him at their house around half eight. No answer at the door, but I found it unlocked, so I announced myself and went in. He was asleep at the kitchen table. He'd been spending the evening with a bottle of Four Roses. I woke him and he asked me to leave. I did."

"What did he say?" asked Weeks.

Buchannon thumbed through his notebook. "Hang on…here it is. I woke him and asked if he was well. He said, 'Piss off.' I asked if he needed any assistance. He said, 'I don't need nothing from you, prat. Now piss off. Get out of me house.' And I did."

Weeks resumed reading from his papers. "Shortly after ten, an anonymous nine-nine-nine call reported a drunk in Treacher's Park."

"A month ago, I brought him in on a drunk and disorderly," said Bennett. "Nicked him at the park. It's just down from his house."

"Yeah," said Buchannon. "He must have got more

of that Four Roses in him and gone out for a stagger. He gets restless."

"There's more," said Weeks. "The caller was out for a late walk and a drunk old man, sitting on the railing, shouted insults as he passed. Then the man fell into the water. The caller ran to the phones by the gazebos and called nine-nine-nine but did not wish to involve themselves further."

Weeks flipped a few more pages. "DS Adams found a hat marked with Pernell Weaver's name on the riverbank, also a pack of cigarettes matching his brand. Cigarette ends from the same pack were found nearby the rail. The river has been high and fast, so anyone falling in would likely be swept away.

"Mr. Weaver was not at his home when we sent officers there. They found a single broken vase. He probably knocked it over, stumbling around the place. He hasn't returned home, nor has he been seen anywhere. The presumption is an accidental death."

He set the folder aside. "Finally, a reminder for the royal wedding. If you aren't on the plainclothes detail, you need to be in your dress blues. Spit spot for telly, everyone."

After one more check of his notes, he said, "That's all I've got. Anyone have anything to add?"

Silence.

"Then let's go," he said. "Watch yourselves." As the room emptied, Weeks motioned for Buchannon to join him at the tea cart. "Mike, a moment."

"Good morning, Roger."

"Can you believe about Weaver?"

"Sadly, yes, I can. Surprised he didn't cash it in years ago."

"My brother at the hospital let the wife know. She's taking it well."

"That's a comfort, anyway," said Buchannon. "Is this all you wanted?"

"No, there's more," said Weeks. "I've started DS Moss keeping tabs on old Walt Lymon."

"You sneaky bastard."

"You watch your manners, young man," said Weeks. "He's spotted Walt's Vauxhall parked on Greenbriar Street. I want you to join him. Work together. Record Walt's habits and maybe we can help Pierce with this theft ring."

"Yeah," said Buchannon. "Or maybe find something new. By the way, is that frame moving along?"

"Yes," said Weeks. "It's at the police yard ready to be released to the owner. Pixley is calling them sometime this morning."

———

The Riley Four-Sixty-Eight headed for Wilbur Estates, council housing at the east end of Dorling. The car radio played the news.

"...and Princess Anne will be wearing a diamond tiara, the very same one Her Majesty The Queen wore at her own wedding in 1947."

Nigel Wilkes shut it off. "Can't drive with this noise. Only thing on the news is the bloody royal wedding."

"Good for the country, though," said Chandler, seated next to him. "It's on telly for the first time, right when it's happening."

"So what?" said Nigel. "Been doing it with the football for ages."

"Surely, this is different than a football broadcast," said Gordon from the back seat.

"Yeah," said Nigel. "It's boring."

"Your generation has no national pride," said

Chandler. "Time to get your head straight, Nigel. We're nearly there."

"Pardon me asking," said Gordon, "but what are we doing?"

Nigel shook his head. Chandler laughed. "Blimey, Jerry, I'm sorry. You've been sitting there all this time sweating about it, eh?"

"Maybe a bit."

"We've got to put the boot to some punks," said Nigel.

Chandler smacked the back of Nigel's head. "Shut it," he said. He shifted his large frame and looked at Jerry Gordon in the back seat.

"There are a number of local businesses Mr. Barnes holds an interest in," he said. "A few of them have made a complaint that needs looking into."

"What sort of 'complaint?'" asked Gordon.

"Shopkeepers being threatened," said Chandler. "Can't have it. Nigel and I will go up and have a chat with the lads who are responsible. Meantime, you'll stay with the car. We may need to leave in a hurry."

"Got it," said Gordon.

———

Raddison's eyes were wide, his lips and gums had a blue cast. "Your intercostal muscles are in spasm," said Marchworth. "It will pass. Try to breathe normally." He checked the connection point between Raddison's catheter and the tube feeding into it.

"This is delivering an agent to your hypothalamus, making it malleable," he said. "When we are finished, it will be nearly prehensile."

"Make it stop," gasped Raddison.

"You have the same potential as anyone who ever lived, but you can't use it. Because your brain does as it pleases. I am giving you control." Marchworth adjusted the rotation speed on the centrifuge. It held fourteen colour-coded test tubes.

Marchworth whispered into his subject's ear. "What you have thought each day is true, Mr. Raddison. You are better than this, and it is not your fault."

VI

Constable Maurice Pixley had excellent phone manners. This morning, it fell to him to contact the owner of a stolen Bentley. "You have it right, Mr. Shipton," he said. "Your car was stripped, I'm afraid. It's called a 'partial recovery.' All we've got is the frame. ...We are certain it is from your car. There is an identification number stamped into the metal. No question at all. ...Yes, your insurance company should call it a total loss. The rest of the parts have likely been sold off. ...Oh, one more thing about this frame—it's yours. That is to say, it's your property and you'll have to claim it. ...No, not identify it. Claim it. Pick it up. Take it away. ...Yes, otherwise I'm afraid the county will charge you for storing it."

An eruption of profanity blasted from the other end of the line. Pixley smiled.

"I understand completely. Many people say the same. ...Well, yes, that's one thing I can do with the frame, but here's another. I'm going to give you the number of a scrap dealer. ...Right, you can take care of this with a phone call. Tell them what's happened, and they'll make you an offer. You'll get a bit of money, and the scrap dealer will come to our yard and pick up what's left of the car. ...Excellent. Do you have a pen, Mr. Shipton?"

A pair of youths stood next to the tombstone sign for Wilbur Estates.

"Hey Nigel," said Chandler, "you see them kids on lookout? Bet that takes you back."

Nigel looked dreamy. "It does."

The car pulled up to the kids with Chandler's window closest. He rolled it down and said, "Excuse me, lads, where can I find Terry Dodds?"

"Sod off, Grandad!" said the skinny eleven-year-old. "Don't know any 'Terry.'"

"Nice manners," said Chandler. "They teach you that at the Borstal school?" He held up a pound note and addressed the other kid. "Your idiot friend just lost a pound. Are you any smarter?"

"He's in his flat. Building D, sixth floor—number nineteen."

Chandler handed over the pound. "Good lad. Don't share it with this twat."

Nigel drove the car to Building D. Some residents milling about the grounds took notice and approached. But as soon as Pat Chandler stepped out of the Riley, he was recognised by all. They walked away, and the car got ignored from then on. "Listen up, Jerry," said Chandler. "Nigel and I are going up to explain things to these people. You get the car pointed toward the road and keep the engine running."

In an unmarked car parked on Greenbriar Street, Detective Sergeant Barry Moss tried to get DI Buchanan to listen. "You're not hearing what I'm telling you," he said.

"I'm not hearing you because I'm trying to hear

the radio," said Buchanan. "I need to know if the Irons won. It's time for sport, but they just keep going on about the bloody wedding."

"Johnny Trillian has gone missing," said Moss.

"I'm not surprised," said Buchannon. "He was seen in our company. He's probably done a runner." He turned down the volume. "Sod it. I'll wait for the papers.

They had been watching Walt Lymon's blue Vauxhall for a while now. Buchannan wondered if Walt was even there. "You know, sometimes you park it and someone else gives you a ride. We might be watching the wrong place while he's off in another car."

"No," said Moss. "He came out of that block of flats earlier. Got something out of his car and went back in."

"Then we wait," said Buchannon. He turned up the volume on the radio.

"…and that's everything in football," said the announcer. "Now, with more on the royal wedding—"

"Bugger," said Buchannon.

———

The pipettes in Doctor Marchworth's hands dripped stabilisers into the last of the fourteen substances he had pulled from Theodore Raddison's brain. Each had been concentrated. Altered. Made better.

Time to put them back in.

Marchworth needed both hands, so he spoke his notes into a microphone on his collar. It was hooked up to a reel-to-reel recorder. "We are three minutes into the reintroduction and the subject has lost consciousness again," he said. "It is probably for the best. His shrieking likely drowned out my previous audio entry. This first phase will be completed soon. Another entry will follow." He stepped on a foot pedal, and the recording stopped.

He prepared the next vial of fluids to be added to Raddison's brain. "Glands, Mr. Raddison," he said. "Invisible hands working your controls. But soon, the control will be yours."

He tapped the side of the vial, making certain the unit held no air. "You will only need to conceive of the feelings and abilities you desire, and your brain will raise or lower dopamine, or corticotrophin. You'll control the production of somatostatin and thyrotropin. You can be as big and strong as you like, or as lean."

He added the contents of the vial to a metal syringe, large enough to be mistaken for a spyglass. "This next phase will decide your future, Mr. Raddison. It will decide all futures."

———

There were five different phone lines in Nick Sanders' office. The center one rang, as he'd been expecting. "Hello, Dorling Scrap and Hauling," he said. "How can I help you? ...A car frame, you say? Yes, we can always use those. Good metal. Can you bring it in or do we need to pick it up? ...I see. Fine, I can bring the paperwork and cash with me. Once I get a look at it, we can do the deal right then and there. ...What's the address, sir? Burnside Road. One one three seven? Hang on, that's the police yard, isn't it? ...Ah, stolen, I see. Yes, we've dealt with those before. ...Right. And your name? ...Got it. When do you think we can get together, Mr. Shipton? ...Let me check...tomorrow near lunch, half eleven? I'll see you at the yard on Burnside." Sanders started filling in his work order.

"My name? Lymon. Walt Lymon. Thank you, Mr. Shipton."

He hung up the phone and scrunched up his nose. "I'm Walt Lymon and I'll see you tomorrow," said Sanders in a dull, low voice. "You can't miss me. I'll be the drunken twit with the enormous, stupid face."

———

DI Buchannon listened to the announcer on the radio, puzzled. "Who is this?"

"Noel Edmonds, he's on the Breakfast Show now. Blackburn's on later."

"I'll give him a chance, as long as he doesn't play that Yellow Ribbon song. Sick of it."

"Yeah," said DS Moss. "It's a tune without merit."

"They play it all day long. I swear, if I hear it again, I'll go down there and hang this Edmonds from an old oak tree."

Moss flipped through a file. "Let's get back to this."

"Can't believe you brought a bloody case file. Fine. You read and I'll keep looking at the Vauxhall. You remember how this is supposed to go, yeah? We look, we watch? Stake things out?"

"But this is about Walt," said Moss. "And Dexter Barnes, and their involvement with the car thefts."

Buchannon shifted in his seat. "Johnny said he hadn't seen them and didn't know anything. Said there was no one around."

"Ah!" said Moss, stabbing a page with his finger. "Got it! Right here in the transcript, 'no one around,' that's what he *said* that he said, but it's not what he said."

"I don't know what *you* just said. How long you been following Walt, anyway?"

"Just a few hours before you joined in. Supposed to find patterns. Record his movements. But he's not made any movements this morning."

Buchannon's stomach growled. "I'll need to make a movement pretty soon."

"We won't be recording your movements."

"I'm going to run into that café and check their plumbing," said Buchannon. "I'll bring back some bacon sandwiches."

"Yeah, fine," said Moss, reaching under his seat. "See if they'll fill this flask with tea."

"Oh certainly, sir," said Buchannon in his high voice. "I'll send the dessert trolley around as well." As he opened his door, he saw Walt Lymon step out of the building.

"Plumbing will have to wait, Mike."

"I hope it can." Buchannon got back into the car as Moss started the engine.

———

After twenty minutes, Chandler and Wilkes returned. Nigel's right hand was wrapped up in a tea towel. Chandler carried a cardboard box.

"You weren't gone long," said Gordon as he opened the car doors. "Is your hand all right?"

"He's fine, just needed ice," said Chandler. "Those Dobbs boys got tough skulls. But we have clarity now, worth the trip. Oh, Nigel, when you make the rounds later, be sure and let the shopkeepers know there's nothing to worry about."

Chandler put the box next to Nigel in the back seat. Then he reached into it and tossed a packet of Walkers crisps to Gordon. Cheese and onion flavour. "Here," he said. "Perks of the trade. Now let's get back to the garage."

———

Theodore Raddison's hands were shaking. His lips trembled, trying to form words around the breathing tube. "With apologies, Mr. Raddison, anything I administer to help with the pain will interfere with the procedure. Your lungs have shut down, but they should start functioning again during phase six."

The bedsheets had soaked through again. Doctor Marchworth pulled his subject to one side and slid a large, absorbent pad under him. "The agony you are experiencing will be worthwhile. Your brain is constructing fresh neural pathways. Of course, this process is causing all of your other systems to cramp and spasm. Bear with me, Mr. Raddison."

VII

At first, Gordon had trouble moving through the gears on the Riley. But after a few miles, he had it going smoothly. "I like the handling on this, Nigel," he said. "How's your hand doing?"

"The ice is all gone, but it's fine. Nothing's broken."

Chandler huffed. "This is why we needed Walt. His hands are like mallets." He shifted in the passenger seat to face Nigel. "You know, Mr. Barnes has been talking about Walt quite a bit lately."

"Is that good?" asked Nigel.

"He's concerned," said Chandler. "Too many times, we haven't been able to track Walt down. Or when he's on a job, he's late and legless. You were with him at Palmer's record shop, right?"

"Yes."

"Palmer has been paying steady for years," said Chandler. "He's been short lately, but it's happened before, and he always catches up."

"Well, to be fair," said Nigel, "Palmer did have a bit of an attitude."

Chandler huffed again. "Walt broke his nose and tossed the place. For a few hundred quid. It's not how Mr. Barnes wants to be known."

"Walt thinks if we lean on a few people harder, we'll have an easier time collecting from the rest," said Nigel.

"'Walt thinks' is a piss poor way to make your point. The man is a blunt object for blunt jobs. And lately, he's unreliable even for that. Full of gin. Wild-eyed on crank. Where is he this morning?"

"I don't know. He's probably waiting for us at the garage by now."

"He's been making time with Molly," said Chandler. "Everyone knows. I think Dex may even know, but he won't say anything as long as she's happy."

Nigel found points of interest outside the car. "That's Walt's business, not mine."

"Bollocks," said Chandler. "And I think the both of you have been doing side work for that nut case out on Boulton Heath. Dexter made it clear he wanted nothing to do with that maniac."

Jerry Gordon did his best to focus on the road. But the Graham Pierce part of him stored mental notes. *Who was Molly? What was out on Boulton Heath? Where was Palmer's record shop?*

"Should we even be discussing this in front of Jerry?" asked Nigel.

"That's a dodge," said Chandler. "And Jerry should hear this, even if it gives him a bit of a squirm. Everyone should understand expectations. And Walt's expected to do his bloody work. If he keeps going the way he's been going, he'll end up having a sit down with Dex. Going to be a lousy day for him *and* me because I'll have to referee the damn thing. If he'll listen to you, tell him to get off the demento-dust and get his work done properly."

————

"He hasn't signalled any of his turns," said DS Moss.

"You want to give him a ticket, Barry?" asked Buchannon.

"Makes it hard to follow him. Maybe that's why he's driving this way."

They'd been tailing Walt Lymon in his blue Vauxhall for miles. "I think he's pissed," said Buchannon. "All over the lanes. He caught a bit of the curb on that last left."

"I'll bet he's headed for Hainsley Road. We'll go straight for a time if he takes it."

Moss was right. They kept a car between theirs and Walt's. Buchannon kept shifting in his seat. "Hope he gets where he's going soon. My condition is getting worse."

"This is just surveillance. I can break it off. We can find him again later."

"No, let's give him a little more line."

————

The more Pat Chandler and Nigel Wilkes argued, the more Gordon wanted out of the car. But the garage was still ten minutes away.

"Look, here's what I'm getting at," said Nigel. "If Walt and me pick up some extra dosh doing side jobs, doesn't it mean Dexter's missed an opportunity?"

Chandler pushed in the dashboard cigarette

lighter. He used it to spark up a Senior Service and put the window down.

"You're right sharp," he said. "So many ways we're doing it wrong. So many ways we'd all have it better if we listened to you." Once again, he turned to Nigel. The two fingers holding his smoke pointed at him. "You listen to me, whelp."

"Wilkes," said Nigel.

"You say 'Wilkes.' I say 'whelp.' So, let me be clear, whelp. You…know…shite."

Nigel opened his mouth, but Chandler kept going. "You may *think* you know how we can do things easier or get more cash. But it's not your house. You can't see how the whole thing works."

He took a deep draw on the Senior Service. No one spoke. Chandler tossed the butt out the window and said, "Dexter, that's Mr. Barnes to you. Built all this up. From birth to ten-years-old, his parents, if you could call them that, had them living in squats all along the East End of London. Nothing to call his, except what he carried. His Mum and the old man robbed and drank or worse, while Dex and his little sister were on their own most of the time. Sometimes for days, and Molly's only six."

While pretending not to listen, Gordon listened intently.

"Mind you, this was the late thirties. The war came on," said Chandler. "During the Blitz, oh, you *do* know what the Blitz is, eh?"

"Yes," said Nigel. "Before my time, but it took my uncle."

"Sorry to hear it," said Chandler. "Well, during the Blitz, Dexter's folks went out one night and never came back. Could have been under a building, maybe they scarpered off. We'll never know. Dex and Molly were found by an ARP Warden. They became orphans of record, though they'd been without parents for ages. Ended up at the Muller Homes, an orphanage out in Ashley Down, near Bristol. That's when we met."

Nigel kept his gaze focused out the window. "You hearing me, son?" asked Chandler.

"Every word, Sir," said Nigel.

"Good," said Chandler. "I'd been there most of my life. Dex arrives, and right away he's running the place. He hustled, made sure Molly was treated well. By the end of his first month, I was running around with him. By the end of the first year, we had a little crew. And I do mean 'little,' we were just kids.

"If we got in trouble, we learned to be more careful. Then we got ahead. And when we got a little older, we got out of there. Eight of us ran off and shared a flat in South London. The oldest was nineteen, so his name went on the papers. We worked hard and earned well, but the real thing we had to bank on was Dexter's charm. Blimey, Dexter at fifteen could talk a Bobbie into loaning him his truncheon.

"And over the last thirty years, he's built all this up. Carefully. And from the bag men to the bookies to the uniforms we pay to look the other way, he's got it structured for one thing—dependability. Not riches, not flash, just steady work for all."

Chandler reached over the seat and tapped Nigel's knee. He waited until Nigel looked at him, then continued.

"You want something bigger? More money? A fat reputation you can wave around like a flag? Fine. If that's your dream, then go bloody make it. Take the risks and make it. But don't for a moment think Mr. Barnes will turn his dream into yours. You hearing me, whelp?"

———

"Your hypothalamus is a musician," said Doctor Marchworth. "The song it plays determines if you are strong or weak. If you are smart or dull. It chooses."

Theodore Raddison hoped he'd pass out again. The breathing tube kept him from speaking. The cramps and spasms kept him from moving. All he could do was lay there and sweat.

And wait.

"I ask you," said Marchworth, "what if you could play any song you like, rather than letting the hypothalamus decide? What if you want to be a genius? Or a strong, brave hero? What if you want to go wild? What if you want a little of one in the morning and a little of the other at night?"

His hand splayed out flat, palm against the back of the syringe's plunger.

"What if you want everything, all at once, right now?"

The doctor's palm jammed the plunger all the way down, forcing every bit of the clear fluid through the syringe, down the tube, and into Raddison's head.

———

"Bugger," said Buchannon. Walt pulled into Dorling Tyre and Auto Repair. "Drive past that garage. Don't slow down. But don't speed up, either."

Moss kept going on Hainsley Road. "Should we come back around? Park across the street?"

"No," said Buchannon. "Just keep going and stop at the first eatery you see." He had seen Graham Pierce standing outside the garage talking with Nigel Wilkes and Pat Chandler. "Good on you, Pierce."

VIII

When the Riley pulled in, Nick Sanders ran to greet Chandler, Gordon, and Wilkes. Partly out of courtesy, but mostly to keep their chatter away from his legitimate clients. He had three cars in the shop, two getting tyres and the other getting tuned. The customers were on benches out front, reading the papers and enjoying complimentary tea and biscuits.

"Good to have you back," said Sanders. "Do I want to know what's in the box?"

"Crisps. Whole lot of Walkers, all kinds," said Nigel. He raised the box chest high. "Where do you want them?"

"Office, for now, I suppose. Thank you. So Pat, your errand went well?"

"All sorted," said Chandler, eyeing Nigel as he struggled into the garage. "Looks like carting a box of snacks is beyond our boy."

"Yes," said Sanders. "Jerry, get over there and help before he hurts himself." Gordon moved. Chandler and Sanders shared a smile.

"Hold on," said Chandler. "Nick's having a laugh, is all."

In less than a minute, Nigel did a half-jog back to the group. "Any word on the frame from the Bentley?"

"All set," said Sanders. "Walt needs to be at the police yard on Burnside tomorrow morning, half eleven. Owner's name is Shipton. You'll need cash and Johnny Trillian with his flatbed."

Nigel gave a little sigh. "Has Walt checked in yet? He needs to know about this."

"Then he needs to be here when he's meant to be,"

said Chandler. "Oh, look at that. 'And he doth appear.'"

The blue Vauxhall pulled into the lot and parked. Walt hopped out of the car, smiling. "Hello, all! How are we this morning?"

———

All of Buchannon's plumbing issues had been sorted. He and Moss sat in a booth, eating their bacon sandwiches. Moss brought the case file with him and read from the transcript of Johnny Trillian's interview. "Look, we're asking him to go over it one more time, right? And he get's all agitated, saying, 'I keep telling you, there was no one around. No one but me.'"

"Yeah. He had to work on one of the rigs, so he stayed late. All alone, he said."

"But it's not what he said. You asked, 'Was anyone else there? Anyone besides you?' Johnny says 'Earlier, yeah. The place was open until six, lots of people about.'"

"I remember," said Buchannon.

"Next bit," said Moss. "You say, 'We're talking about later, after midnight. Was there anyone else there besides you?'"

"And what did he say?"

Moss read slowly. "Hang on, here it is. 'Thought I heard something, so I checked the alley and the gates around ten and didn't see anyone. Got to be careful. We were robbed last month, and you lot have done a shite job of catching them.'"

"Prat got to me, didn't he," said Buchannon.

"Yeah. The both of you argue a bit, then move on," said Moss, closing the file. "He never answered the question. He said there were a lot of people in there until they closed, then a few hours later he checked around and made sure they were locked up and didn't see anyone. But he never said, specifically, he was the only one there after midnight."

"Got to listen to what they *don't* say. Even closer than you listen to what they *do* say. If he's being so evasive, you can be sure someone was there. Someone he doesn't want us to know about."

"Someone like Walt Lymon," said Moss.

"Be a good idea to bring Johnny back in, eh?"

"Love to," said Moss, trying to get the bacon off his hands with a tiny paper napkin. "But like I told you, no one has seen him."

"Either he's done a runner, or he should have."

———

It took a good deal of tugging to remove the breathing tube from Raddison. His convulsing muscles didn't want to let it go.

Once it came out, he gagged and coughed as he tried to speak. The words were unintelligible. Doctor Marchworth used a clean, warm towel to wipe his subject's mouth and face. Raddison stared at him, wild-eyed, gasping. "Breathing on your own again," said Marchworth. "This is progress."

Six of the machines monitoring Raddison's condition were outfitted with alarms, and all of them were going off.

"I apologise for the noise, Mr. Raddison." Marchworth moved around the room, disabling the alarms. He knew full well his patient was in crisis. The cacophony provided no new data.

Marchworth made note of the swollen areas of his subject's face and head, a side effect of the glandular disruptions during this phase of the treatment. He saw a tremor in Raddison's legs and got the restraints tightened just as a violent seizure shook his subject hard enough to make the bed move.

Raddison let out a shrill vibrato scream as the doctor eased more fluids into his head.

———

Nigel and Walt let it be known they'd lost their flatbed driver, Johnny Trillian. Chandler looked skyward, thinking. Then he instructed Gordon to walk away. Once he was out of earshot, an animated discussion began.

Pouring himself some tea where the customers were sitting, Gordon still heard the men yelling. "What's that about?" asked a woman in a flower dress.

"Selling a car, I think," said Gordon. "Disagreement on the price."

He went inside and pulled on his coveralls. There was a Beetle waiting for new tyres. Gordon started loosening the nuts on the old ones when Sanders appeared. "Jerry, a moment please," he said.

"I've only just started, Mr. Sanders."

"Call me Nick. And we can get Lionel to take over." Sanders' gaze swept the shop. "Say, where is Lionel?"

"I'm right here," said Lionel Barris, standing next to Sanders.

"Oh, there you are. Take over for Gordon, will you?"

When he wasn't working on cars, Lionel Barris was the best burglar around. In the house where he grew up, there was only one way to stay out of danger with the old man. You had to be invisible. Never get noticed.

It became second nature and followed him into

adulthood. Lionel could sneak in and out of any-where without being seen.

Sanders led Gordon to the alley behind the shop, where they kept a flatbed. "Jerry, can you drive this? And run the winch and the liftgate and all?"

"Yes."

"Good. Come with me," said Sanders. "Doesn't look like you're going to work on many cars today."

———

"I'm going to wash my hands, then we can get out of here," said DS Moss.

"Fine," said Buchannon. "I'll pay and meet you up front."

Moss reached for his wallet. "Stop it, Barry. You'll get your pockets all porky. You can get the next one."

At the front counter, Buchannon paid the check. Lunch hour loomed, and the café had got busy. Moss joined him minutes later, hands free of bacon leav-ings. "Are we paid up?"

"We are," said Buchannon. "Let's see if we can find that twat Walt Lymon." They turned to find three ladies behind them, waiting for their table. There were holding a few gifts and some flowers.

The youngest of them was in her sixties. She scolded the men. "We'll thank you to keep that sort of talk quiet," she said. "It's Diedre's birthday today."

"Pardon me," said Buchannon. "Sorry, Ma'am."

He and Moss wove their way to the door. Then they heard laughter. Gentle laughter, like children playing with soap bubbles, but the voices were older.

They turned and saw that the ladies had dropped the gifts and flowers. They had also dropped their clothes.

They looked like The Three Graces. The statue had

fascinated Barry Moss in secondary school, and now it had come to life. The three of them, naked, moving around each other in a tight circle. Some bystanders moved back, looked away. A few came forward, offered help. A waitress approached with a stack of towels. "Ladies, please cover yourselves," she said.

The ladies paid no mind. Joyfully, they twirled in a tight loop, one after the other. A game of geriatric follow-the-leader, with the boundaries set between the lunch counter and the tables.

After a few minutes, the ladies' bliss got interrupted by a policeman who had been summoned from up the street.

He tried to contain the situation, fumbling with the towels and his coat. The poor man was soon overwhelmed by a complete lack of training for this sort of thing and his shyness regarding the female form, regardless of age.

Buchannon tilted his head toward the trouble. Moss nodded. Both officers showed their identification and joined the policeman. No longer outnumbered by the delighted, nude pensioners, he got the situation under control.

A crowd had gathered by the time the police van arrived. They booed as the ladies were loaded up and taken away.

IX

"Christ! Nasty thing," said Nigel, examining his hand.

"Same one you hurt earlier, isn't it?" asked Gordon.

"Yes, it is," said Nigel. "And it's fine, just a sliver."

A pair of work gloves bounced off his face. "Hey! Watch it!"

Walt had tossed the gloves. "How many times have I told you to wear gloves when you're dealing with these crates? Now, let's load these last two and get moving."

The three of them were at a row of lockups near the garage, where Sanders stored stacks of tyres, cans of fluids, and car parts.

They were moving crates out of the middle unit. All the crates were stenciled with numbers and the word "BENTLEY." Some were heavy enough to merit using the winch, but most made their way onto the flatbed with a hand truck.

The part of Gordon's brain belonging to DS Graham Pierce knew he'd found the rest of the stolen Bentley. But he still didn't understand how this enterprise worked, so he kept quiet and moved crates. Soon, everything was tied down neatly, and they hauled it all back to the garage.

———

At home that evening, Graham Pierce leaned against a heating pad as he ate his Chinese takeaway. The noodles were salty with lots of water chestnuts. Just the thing he needed to help him think.

What would he say if Buchannon brought up the trouble with his newsagent's? He probably wouldn't, didn't sound interested last night. But what bothered Pierce was the police's inability to help the situation.

If the Hamadi's were injured or their store damaged, then they could make inquiries. But isn't that too late?

Dexter Barnes' people got it dealt with. Direct, effective, and no cost to the taxpayer.

Pierce noticed parallels between working for Dexter Barnes and working for Dorling CID. Their methods were different, but they were after the same things. Both groups wanted better pay and perks. Both wanted peaceful outcomes to conflicts.

Both were wary of betrayers. The people on Dexter's side were looking for informants and the people at the nick were looking for bent cops. Again, same motivation, different methods.

And gossip at Dorling Tyre and Auto Repair flowed at the same frantic rate as gossip at the Dorling CID canteen.

His phone rang. Time for some gossip with DI Buchannon.

———

There hadn't been a violent seizure in hours, but Raddison continued to shake as if stricken with palsy. He'd lost consciousness again. Marchworth noted his belief these lapses were useful to the brain as it "felt along the new pathways."

He lifted Raddison's eyelids. The pupils extended past the iris and the sclera had become glossy. There were no colours anymore, just white and black. They were eyes like you'd see on a puppet.

His previous subject had the opposite manifestation. Her pupils became pinpoints. The autopsy revealed atrophy of the optic nerve. In fact, the subject developed complete facial paralysis in the days leading to her death.

He took his journal to the chair by the fire. He intended to organise his notes, but he'd been working for days and it caught up to him all at once. Doctor Marchworth fell asleep.

DI Buchannon was nearly through his page of topics to cover with Pierce.

"Weeks cancelled the surveillance," he said. "Figured you were keeping tabs on Walt Lymon already and he didn't want to blow your cover."

"Spent most of the day with Walt," said Pierce. He switched the handset to his other ear. "Probably tomorrow as well. I'm working that night thing and they've got me driving their flatbed. I'll be picking up the stolen frame from the police yard."

"Moving up in the world," said Buchannon. "This building where Walt spent the morning is where Molly Colbert lives. She used to be Molly Barnes."

"Dexter's sister," said Pierce.

"She got married to a Luc Colbert ten years ago. Legit bloke. Worked in a bank. They lived in Paris," said Buchannon. "He died in a car crash and she came to Dorling to be close to family. Runs a shop for leather goods in town. Sells handbags and boots."

"They said Walt's been making time with her. Said it wouldn't sit well with Dexter Barnes."

"I'll bet," said Buchannon. "On your other items, we'll look into Boulton Heath. There's only the one house out there. Belongs to the Marchworth family."

"Okay. Careful, though, Chandler said the resident was a maniac."

"We'll go slowly."

"Good. And what about this Palmer person?" said Pierce. "Got knocked about for being short on his collections?"

"Probably Jamie Palmer. Runs that record shop, The Melody Market. Been moving swag out the back door for ages, but we can't make anything stick. He'll have an interesting story about how he broke his nose, but it won't involve Walt."

"Got it," said Pierce. "That's all I had. You got anything else?"

"No," said Buchannon. "Since you're going late tomorrow, I'll leave you to it for the next few days. Call the station and leave me a time when we can talk. I'll make it work."

"Right," said Pierce. "Oh, you had any more of those naked troublemakers?"

"Just today. I'll fill you in when we've got more time. You watch yourself."

"I will," said Pierce. "You be careful as well."

The job of acquiring the frame from the police yard went well. Jerry Gordon drove the flatbed. Walt and Nigel were punctual, and Mr. Shipton was happy with the money.

Lionel had come along to help with the loading, and the set of extra hands made the process smooth. The flatbed delivered the Bentley's skeleton to Dorling Tyre and Auto Repair in time for a late lunch.

Walt and Nigel went off to deal with other matters. "Real work is in the offing," said Sanders. "It means those two will stay far away."

"This is a relief," said Gordon. "I was worried I'd signed onto something shady tonight, like stripping a car."

"Just the opposite," said Sanders. "We're putting a car together."

Roger Weeks looked over the notes, maps, and records pinned on the board in the briefing room. Moss and Buchannon had been thorough.

"All the way out on Boulton Heath," said Weeks. "I thought the place was vacant."

"It was until just over a year ago," said Moss. "He may have been their longer, but that's when the council filled an order to get more electricity to the house. New line, new panel, requested and paid for by the resident."

Buchannon pointed at a copy of the work order on the board. "Name on the form is Doctor Fredrick Marchworth. Records show he's the only son, forty-seven. He's likely the last of the line."

"He'd be the only person around for miles," said Weeks. "No one lives out there since the Terrandale Marshes rose up. Houses are sinking and the bugs will eat you alive."

"His place is solid. Power, water, phone, all the modern conveniences. And the road is in good shape," said Moss. "The council got their lorries in and out, no problems."

"So, he's forty-seven, and he likes electricity," said Weeks. "What else do we know about Doctor Frederick Marchworth?"

"He's rich," said Moss. "Family has always been well off and he's got it all now. For years, he was a researcher at Oxford Medical School. Wrote a few papers. That's a family thing, they made their money with patents on medical equipment."

"I made a few calls to Oxford," said Buchannon. "He left on good terms. He's gone off to do some research on his own and write a book or some such thing."

"Okay," said Weeks. "He's out there working on a textbook or something. But what the hell is old Walt

Lymon doing for him? He doesn't strike me as the scientific type."

"Yeah," said Moss. "And how horrid a person do you have to be for Dexter Barnes to call you a 'maniac?'"

"I think you two should find out," said Weeks.

———

Once the garage had closed for the day, the crew stayed on for another hour. They hassled the frame off the flatbed and positioned it on the center lift. Next, the crates stenciled BENTLEY were opened.

They contained the rest of the vehicle. Using the factory guides and a notebook of handwritten instructions (complete with snapshots of this car's disassembly), they staged the panels and parts on worktables and rolling carts all around the frame.

It was as if someone had taken an Airfix model kit for a Bentley T1 Coupé and blown it up to life-size. With everything staged, Sanders sent his crew home with an extra tenner for each.

Pierce still didn't understand. Why steal a car, disassemble it, and store the parts rather than sell them? Then, weeks later, you reacquire the frame and do the whole thing again in reverse. It's all work and no money.

No, keep your mouth shut, he thought. *Wait and watch. Barnes is smart, smarter than most. There's no way he'd be doing this if there wasn't a profit.*

"All right, Gordon," said Sanders. "You and I will read through the procedures, top to bottom. Make certain we have what's needed. Lionel, you run down to the chip shop and get us something to eat."

"Cheers," said Lionel. Pierce hadn't realised Lionel was still there.

X

His fingers stopped bending properly years ago, which made dialing the payphone awkward for Walt. The headlights from the Vauxhall lit the booth but hurt his head.

Nigel waited in the car, dozing. It had been a trying day, and he hoped this was their last call.

The phone woke Doctor Marchworth. His eyes leapt to the clock. He'd been asleep for hours. He rushed to the medical area, scanned the monitors, and checked Raddison's vital signs.

No changes.

The phone kept ringing. Marchworth engaged the intercom. "Yes?" he said.

"Hello Professor! Walt Lymon here. Am I coming through all right? You sound fuzzy."

"I can hear you clearly, Mr. Lymon. Why have you called?"

"Just checking in. We haven't spoke since our last visit."

Marchworth shook his head. "We have not spoken because we do not need to. You have been paid and I am working."

"I see," said Walt. "Sound like this one's hanging on, then."

"Yes," said Marchworth. "Hanging on."

"Well, if you should need a disposal or another, er, what did you call it?"

"Acquisition," said Marchworth.

"Yes, 'acquisition.' Well, you know how to find me."

"Goodbye Mr. Lymon."

"Goodbye. Thanks, Professor!" Nigel got his wish. They weren't needed at Marchworth's.

The doctor switched off the intercom and returned to the chair to gather his notes.

He heard laughter. It was Theodore Raddison.

———

Just when the work got heavy, a beaten old Morris Minor pulled up to the garage.

Out poured a rowdy bunch in skinny jeans and wild hair. The Divers Hands had arrived.

Gordon clocked six young people. They each looked about seventeen years old.

Sanders greeted them at the entrance. They were all racket, piss, and chaos. "Shut your noise," he said, blocking their way. "Martin, get this lot organised or I'll send you right along."

"Got it," shouted Martin. "Hey, you lot, get organised or we'll be sent right along."

Silence. Attention. Stillness.

Martin Reynolds was clearly the one in charge.

"Better," said Sanders. "Listen up, there's nothing new happening tonight. Same work you've done before. In fact, I think we did one just like this a few months ago."

"Just like?" said Martin. "Pretty sure this is the same one."

"Blimey, you're right. It might be," said Sanders. That got a laugh all around. Sanders handed Martin a stack of five-pound notes to distribute among his people.

"Line up, you know how this works," said Martin, giving a fiver to each. "One now and more as you go. Let's get on it."

Two girls, four boys, with Martin riding herd. They worked in singles and pairs, grabbing panels, parts, and tools in a well-coordinated scramble that wouldn't be out of place as a variety show act.

Sanders put his hand on Gordon's shoulder. "This is our tea break," he said. "Wash up and I'll pop the kettle on."

———

Moss and Buchannon were settling into their car. "You sure about the directions?" asked Moss.

"Yes," said Buchannon. "Besides, this is a radio car. We can call in if we get turned around."

"The road isn't lit out there. And this talk of a maniac has me on edge."

"Just start the engine. Boulton Heath is more than an hour away. You can build up your courage along the route."

———

Raddison spoke in bursts, ignoring questions and instructions from Doctor Marchworth. He had a twice-normal pulse. The intravenous fluids barely kept pace with the sweats. His extremities still tremored, chafing against the restraints. If Raddison didn't break through these symptoms, he'd join the other failures in death.

"Your alpha waves are beyond this machine's ability to measure," said Marchworth. "I have never been closer. Tell me everything."

"The act of grabbing a cup or flipping on a light happens in the absence of thought," said Raddison. "The act is simply done."

Marchworth frowned. "What? You have more mental power than anyone alive and you are raving. Focus. Tell me your thoughts."

Raddison's words came even faster. "I *am* telling you, but you can't understand."

———

"It's a good crew, these kids," said Sanders. "They do all kinds of one-off jobs for Mr. Barnes."

"Can't fault their energy," said Gordon.

"Martin came up with that blasted name, insists on everyone calling them 'The Divers Hands.' There's nothing they can't do, as long as you've got a stack of fivers to toss at them. They'll have the heavy stuff finished on the Coupé in short order."

Gordon drained his tea. "What's our part, then?"

"Lionel keeps The Divers Hands moving down the checklist. You and I will do the fine work," said Sanders. "I don't trust any of those kids to use a torque wrench properly, or to set up the fuses. Two of them, Ellen and Darryl, they do the welds. Better than me, they are. Neat and quick. When they're done, we'll start the precision bits, foot-pounds and amperages and the like."

"Sounds like I should start measuring out the wires," said Gordon.

"Good lad," said Sanders. "Off you go. I'll find the diagrams, so we're ready to lay it in."

———

"Reach, do you hear me? Reach," said Raddison. "It's not about thinking, it's about *reach*.

"Yes?" Doctor Marchworth had started the tape recorder. "What about 'reach?'"

"Reach is assumed to have limits. But when you know, when you are certain your reach extends beyond your skin, that's when all things become possible."

"It sounds as if you have gained an understanding, Mr. Raddison."

"Yes," said Raddison. "But you can't think about it. Needs to be mindless, like scratching your ear or tapping your fingers. No concentration, just the act. Autonomous."

"Are you thirsty, Mr. Raddison?" asked Marchworth. "Perhaps some apple juice."

"No." Raddison's voice became clear and sharp. "I'm close. Soon, maybe in another hour, I will be able to move the lamp to your right. Or I'll shake this table or tug your coat."

"You will escape these restraints?"

"No, I will use thoughts. But I need to do it the same way I move my fingers. Without thinking. This is the paradox I'm breaking through."

Doctor Marchworth considered another injection of testosterone.

"You don't need to jam more potions into my brain," said Raddison. "I'm making the stuff on my own. You aren't creating evolution anymore. You are in its way."

Marchworth stepped away from the bed.

"You've succeeded, doctor," said Raddison. "I'm becoming your superior being. I can feel it. And you are correct about these restraints. Soon, I'll drop them on the floor. But first I will kill you. It's coming. It's coming soon."

———

Buchannon pointed to the rise ahead. "There, you can see the lights are on. That's the Marchworth house."

"Big place," said Moss, peering over the wheel. "Where do you think I turn to get up there?"

"Should be a private road on the right. No gate, just winds up to a parking circle in front of the place."

"Before we knock, we should hop on the radio and make sure they can hear it back at CID."

"A wise and cautious plan," said Buchannon. "Glad you're along on this one, DS Moss."

"Nowhere I'd rather be, DI Buchannon. And that is what it sounds like when I'm telling porkies."

———

Pierce knew he'd be pulling an all-nighter, but he didn't know it would be a joy. The energy, the high spirits, the teamwork in the garage took him all the way back to camp-outs with the Scouts in his youth.

He'd be dropping by The Melody Market tomorrow. The Hands were playing an album by Desmond Dekker over and over, and Pierce had to own it.

———

Theodore Raddison's breathing grew stronger. His pulse still ran fast, and the sweats continued. "I can't see the future," he said. "I do not have precognition. Yet, I know I'm going to kill you, Marchworth."

The doctor checked the levels in the IV bottles. "How will you manage that, Mr. Raddison?"

Raddison laughed. "The moment I 'gain understanding,' as you say. Precisely then, I will crush your heart. Or maybe wring your brain. And once you're lifeless on the floor, I'll be able to see clearly. Right now, your death clouds my vision. It's all I can see."

Fear crept over Marchworth, a danger to his objectivity. "It sounds as if I may have learned all I can from you," he said.

"You are scared of me," said Raddison. "I can smell it. But can you bring yourself to destroy me? Can you stop when you're so close to success?"

"The process cannot be called 'successful' unless it can be repeated," said Marchworth. "I have the data from these monitors, my notes, and the audio recordings. All that, along with the findings from your autopsy, will become the baseline for my next subject."

"You mean your next victim," said Raddison.

"Call it what you will," said Marchworth. "This portion of my research is complete."

The doctor twisted a valve and the intravenous pump switched bottles. Pink fluid moved into Raddison's veins. His body convulsed and sweat formed a fine mist all around him, soaking the bed.

Marchworth examined the monitors. "Odd," he said. He checked the vital signs. Blood pressure, pulse, respiration, all showed the man was dead.

Yet the alpha waves continued. Strong. Raddison's brain was active.

"What dreams may come, indeed?" said Marchworth.

The bell rang at the front door. He heard muted voices.

"Hello? Doctor Marchworth? Frederick Marchworth? We're from Dorling CID. Apologies for the late hour, but can you open the door, please?"

XI

The phone pulled Dexter Barnes out of a dead sleep. Calls this late were never good news.

"Hello," he said. "Molly? Molly, what's happened? ...Is anyone there or are you alone? ...Don't answer the door to anyone but me and don't go anywhere. I'll be right over."

Barnes hung up the phone. "Bastard," he said.

Marchworth stood silently in his entryway, waiting to hear the police officers go away. He remained still, hoping they would think the house deserted.

The bell rang again, along with vigorous knocking. "Doctor Marchworth? Are you there? It's the police."

The officers waited. "What do you think, Mike?" asked Moss.

"It's a big house," said Buchannon. "Do we need to be louder?"

Both officers jumped as the door's massive deadbolt rolled over. They heard a chain lock move. "Guess he's home after all," said Moss.

Inside, Doctor Marchworth used all of his strength to twist the deadbolt back the other way, but an unseen force held it open. He scarcely believed his eyes as the chain lock slid from its groove and dropped on its own.

"Mr. Raddison," he whispered. "Is this your doing? The most powerful being on Earth and you are performing magic tricks?"

The door swung open, nearly hitting Marchworth in the face.

"Ah, good evening," said Moss. "You must be Doctor Marchworth."

Keeping a calm front, Doctor Marchworth began his reply. Before he could speak, a voice cried out from the other room.

"Help! Help me, please!"

Buchannon grabbed Marchworth as Moss ran inside.

"Stay with me, Doctor," said Buchannon. "Who is that?" Marchworth felt an odd pressure rising in his chest. He couldn't speak.

Moss ran past the door on his way to the car. "Cuff him, Mike. He's got a man tied to a bed in there. Tubes, chemicals, it's terrible. I'm calling for an ambulance and backup."

Theodore Raddison continued pressing the doctor's heart, but permitted him to speak.

"You must take me," said Marchworth, his voice strained.

Buchannon cuffed him and put in the back of the car. Once they were away from the house, the pain in Marchworth's chest subsided. "So," he said, "you have a range."

"What did you say?" asked Buchannon.

"It is no concern of yours, detective."

In the front seat, Moss had just finished his radio calls. "Ambulance is en route from Terrandale Hospital," he said. "They were closest, but it's still twenty minutes. Backup is on the way as well."

"I'll have a talk with the doctor," said Buchannon. "Go see if you can help that man."

"Right," said Moss. He returned to the house. Marchworth stared straight ahead.

"This man in the other room," said Buchannon. "Will he live?"

The doctor considered the question carefully. "He will do so much more."

———

Sanders used a clean towel to work out the last smack of wax on the Bentley's rear bumper. The road test went well, this detail work was the last step.

Everyone did an orbit around the car, making certain nothing got missed.

"Who done the paint?" asked Ellen. "It's lovely."

"Warren Bright over at Bright Carworks," said Sanders. "It's a factory colour, nice dark green."

"Is that another of Mr. Barnes' shops?"

"Yes," said Sanders. "He owns a lot of car places."

"Well, it's just lovely," said Ellen.

"Yeah," said Martin. "I'm like to bust out crying. Are we done, Mr. Sanders? Anything else we can do for you?"

"Don't think so. Hey Lionel, go get…where's Lionel?"

"I'm right here," said Lionel.

"Ah, there you are. Go get the box of Walkers out the office." Lionel ran up while Sanders did a last look around the shop. "Yes. It's a good result and everything is stored away tidy." He handed Martin another stack of five-pound notes as Lionel returned with the box and handed it to Darryl.

"Walkers Crisps, all sorts," said Lionel. "I'm sure you can find use for those."

Martin and his crew looked more excited by the snacks than the money. "Yes," said Martin. "We will give every packet a good home. Divers Hands, to the Morris!"

Just as when they arrived, The Hands were all racket, piss, and chaos as they tumbled into the Morris Minor and roared away.

That left Lionel, Gordon, and Sanders. "It's late. Lionel, are you safe to drive home?" asked Sanders.

"Just two miles," said Lionel. "When do you want me back?"

"Got the head gasket on the Mercedes tomorrow," said Sanders, handing over a stack of money. "Can you do eleven?"

"You won't even know I was gone," said Lionel. And with that, he disappeared.

Sanders turned to Gordon, handing him a stack of money as well. "You and I are to wait here with the car. A carrier is coming from London. There's a couch in the office if you need a lie down."

"Good idea," said Gordon. He fell asleep with Desmond Dekker singing, *You Can Get It If You Really Want*, in his head.

———

The house on Boulton Heath had become more populated than it had been in years. Scenes of Crime Officers were covering every inch of the place. Emmie Firmin was in charge. She'd been heading up this team for five years now.

She stepped out of the caution-taped area for a cigarette. DI Mike Buchannon joined her. "Been at this for decades," he said. "Never seen anything like this."

"Nor I," said Firmin. "The doctor, did he talk?"

"A little. He's responsible for our missing tramps. He called them 'broken people.' Said he was distilling them, using the result to help us all. To change the world. Moss took him to the station. Don't know what he's said since."

"How many people are missing?" she asked.

"Hard to say. With this group, many are likely unreported. At least five."

"Any word on the man they found in the bed? The one they took to hospital?"

"He's hanging on. I don't even know his name. Lord knows what the mad bugger did to him."

Emmie Firmin put out her cigarette under her shoe. "His name is Theodore Raddison. And we know precisely what the mad bugger did to him. Come with me."

———

Graham Pierce woke slowly, unsure of his surroundings. There were voices. Gray light in the window told him the sun was just coming up.

Not Pierce, he thought. *I'm Jerry Gordon.*

Though he'd only slept a few dreamless hours, he felt rested. Looking forward to the day running with Barnes' crew.

And hopefully, the last piece in this car theft puzzle would drop into place. A bright morning in both his worlds.

The thought stopped him. He didn't have two worlds; he was a policeman. And these were crooks. No, don't get too close. Don't fall into the good times and flash. Don't make friends.

Sanders had suggested he bring a clean shirt and a shaving kit, and Gordon had done so. He got cleaned up and made his way to the gravel outside the garage just as the Bentley rolled onto the carrier.

Last night, a scattering of parts. Now, the gleaming touchstone of British luxury.

He felt pride.

"Jerry, come over here." It was Pat Chandler, standing in the doorway. They walked together to a folding table at the back of the shop, laid out with tea and pastries. "Fortify yourself. That was a good night's work. The ones with cheese on top have egg and sausage inside. Start with those."

Gordon took a big bite. Wonderful.

"Did you bring these, Mr. Chandler? Thank you."

"I didn't bring them, I had them brought. Get that in you. Then wash your hands. Then find me outside."

Gordon did just that. Outside, he got a last look at the Coupé as it went under a canvas cover. The carrier had a logo on the door, *Prestige Motors, Ltd.* Seeing the logo, he finally understood the entire enterprise.

Prestige Motors was a major dealer in luxury cars. They'd sell a vehicle and Barnes would have it stolen, then carefully dismantled.

Once the exterior components were painted a different colour, everything went into storage. After a time, a large piece is recovered, one the owner wouldn't be interested in keeping. The car is considered a total loss, and on paper, no longer exists.

The large piece gets purchased for a scrap fee, then the car is reassembled. Prestige Motors must be in league with someone at the DVLA who refreshes the registration and number plates.

Free car.

They weren't selling off parts. They were selling the same vehicle again and again, as if it were new.

"Looks nice," said Chandler, approaching. He pointed to a group of men in front of the carrier. "They've about finished," he said. "When they have, I want you to meet Mr. Barnes. He's the one with the mustache."

Until that moment, Pierce had only seen Dexter Barnes in a series of grainy photos pinned up on a board. Certain facts were known: He lived here in Dorling, but his criminal network stretched across England. He had a nice but unassuming house by the river. He drove a sturdy, old Range Rover.

This morning, he wore a simple dark suit and overcoat. No sharkskin or spectator shoes. No pinky rings. If someone had offered you a hundred pounds to guess his occupation, "crime boss" would never come to mind. He looked like a bank manager.

As the group around Barnes shared a laugh, Pat Chandler caught his eye. Barnes excused himself and trotted across the gravel. "Dexter, this is Jerry Gordon," said Chandler. "The one I told you about."

"Ah," said Barnes, smiling. "Fresh from Brixton, I understand. Good to meet you." He extended his hand.

Pierce got this undercover assignment to gather evidence about a car theft ring and to gain as much intel as possible about Dexter Barnes. Outsiders couldn't get near him.

He shook the man's hand. "Nice to meet you, Mr. Barnes."

"Sanders tells me you did a lot of the work on the Bentley," said Barnes.

"Everyone did a lot of work on the Bentley, Sir. Those side panels were real knuckle busters. Turned out pretty, though."

"Yes, very pretty." Barnes turned his attention to Chandler. "Oh Pat; do I need to worry about that other thing?"

"You don't have to worry about it," he said. "It's next on my list."

"Good. Take Gordon, here." Barnes called to Sanders. "Hey Sanders, you mind if Pat borrows this man for the morning?"

"Do what you like with him," said Sanders. "He's got the day off."

Barnes put his hand on Gordon's shoulder. "There you are. Extra money on your day off. Never a bad thing, is it?"

"No sir. I can always use the work."

"Good. See you around, Jerry Gordon." Dexter Barnes returned to the group by the Bentley.

"Looks like you're running the flatbed for me this morning.," said Chandler.

"Can do," said Gordon. "Just have to make a quick phone call, if I may. I'm supposed to meet a friend this morning and I need to cancel it."

"Fine," said Chandler. "And have another one of those pastries. We have a long drive ahead."

XII

Emmie Fermin led DI Mike Buchannon through a long hall to a run of old stairs. They ended up in a stone chamber, down the hill from the Marchworth home. "This is an icehouse," she said. "The place is old, but he's got this all lit and clean."

File cases and wire shelves stacked with jars formed a maze through the place. "What is all this?" asked Buchannon.

"We're still going through it," said Firmin. "He's typed everything up. Victims' names, ages. Each procedure. Catalogued the lot. The pathologist needs time. Going to be a long study."

Buchannon reached toward a jar on one of the shelves.

"Please, don't touch anything," said Firmin. "It looks like a natural history museum, the way he's got it all organized and tagged. So tidy. This is a workplace. Dark work. These missing persons, they were specimens to him."

"Just guinea pigs," said Buchannon. "It's awful to think of."

"Near as I can tell, there's fifteen people," said Firmin. "Each one gets a number, and those numbers are on the jars. These optic nerves in jar seven belong to the brain over there on the tall shelf, also number seven. There are parts with the same number all around, like ghastly puzzle pieces. And just parts."

"Just parts? What does that mean?"

"We haven't found any corpses yet," said Fermin. "Just smaller parts that were harvested from them."

A uniformed officer appeared at the entrance. "DI Buchannon? You in here?"

"Back here," said Buchannon.

"Blimey," said the officer, taking in the scene.

"Yes, it's terrible," said Buchannon. "What did you need?"

"Oh, sorry Sir. Call for you on the radio, patched from the station. Sent me to find you. It's important, something about cars."

———

"There," said Chandler, seated on the passenger side of the flatbed. "The car in the middle with the cover over it." They had pulled into a car park well outside of Dorling.

Gordon backed the flatbed up to the car and pulled off the cover. Chandler tossed him a set of keys. "Hook it up, then put the cover back on."

It was Walt's blue Vauxhall.

"I'm growing to trust you, Jerry," said Chandler. "You should know what's happened."

"If you think so, Sir."

"While you were working on the Bentley last night," said Chandler, lighting a Senior Service, "Walt was out drinking and drugging. He ended up at Molly's place. That's Mr. Barnes' sister. And she's a doll."

Gordon listened and busied himself feeding out the cable from the winch.

"She had some people over, and it really got on his

wick. Walt didn't like the way she acted. Didn't like anyone there. He pounds the table, knocks drinks over, makes a scene. Then he kicks everybody out. It's not even his flat. Then it's just her and him, and they have a row."

Chandler stubbed out his cigarette and spat. "He hits her, then storms off."

Silence.

"I don't think that's the end of it," said Gordon.

"No," said Chandler. "Molly called her brother."

"Mr. Barnes."

"The same. Dex comes right over and there's Molly crying with a split lip, dabbing it with Brulidine. She bends Dex's ear about Walt. He planned on having a word with Walt about his behaviour problems anyway, but this pushed things right off the edge."

Gordon pulled the lever, and the Vauxhall rolled onto the bed.

"Dex collected me and some trusted mates. We went out looking for old Walt," said Chandler. "Found him scoring crank in an alley off March Street. Them he was with scattered when they saw Dexter's car, and he sent me and the boys to bring Walt over.

"Walt, being full of Tetley's and gin and crank, he set himself up. Raised his fists and got in this wobbly stance."

"Christ," said Gordon.

"He called Dexter out," said Chandler. "Yelled down the alley, saying Dex was too scared to fight on his own. The bastard just beat on a girl half his size and he's calling Dex a coward. That rung Dexter's bell. He mashed down on the gas and ran Walt over."

"Ran him over?" asked Gordon, covering the car.

"Well, not *over*," said Chandler. "The front end pushed him up against the wall. Popped his spine and banged his head on the bricks. The end for old Walt. The boys got the alley cleaned up. Dexter told Molly he ran Walt off. Told him to leave town, never come back, and good riddance."

"Well, he's right. Walt won't be coming back," said Gordon, pulling the last tie-down.

"You don't know how right you are," said Chandler. "He's in the boot of that Vauxhall. We're taking him and his damn car to the garden."

"Where's that?"

"Out in The Fens."

————

Moss and Buchannon got a few hours' sleep but were soon back on the job. They drove around town looking for Walt Lymon and Nigel Wilkes.

"For someone who likes being seen, Walt sure is hard to find today," said DS Moss.

"The papers from Marchworth's place made it clear," said Buchannon. "Those two provided the people for the doctor to work on. Makes me sick just saying it."

"They picked up the remains, as well. Like they were ragmen. Fifteen people."

The radio sputtered. "Two-two-five, calling out for two-two-five. Mike? Are you there?"

Buchannan grabbed the handpiece. "This is DI Mike Buchannon responding, over."

"It's Roger," said the voice on the radio. "Any sign of them yet?"

"None."

"You two should come back to the station. Something is happening."

————

Gladdom's Bloom Farm, out in The Fens, was the largest producer of cut flowers in England. In addition to their own shops, they supplied sellers and specialty venues all over Europe. Acres and acres of budding plants amongst the peat, all owned by the Gladdom family. It was one of England's first recorded deeds.

Walt Lymon and his Vauxhall would arrive there in another twenty minutes.

Pat Chandler watched the countryside fly past his window. "Do you want to know more?" he asked.

"Should I know more?" asked Gordon.

"Well, I'd rather fill you in now than field questions once we're there doing business." Chandler shifted to his left. "Forgot how much these bench seats aggravate my back."

"There's a little pillow underneath. Sanders uses it."

Chandler found the pillow and stuffed it behind him. "Better, thank you." He lit a cigarette and put down the window. "Here's what you need to know. At some point in their lives, everyone in the world has murder cross their minds. Your mum, the Vicar, everyone. Passes quickly, for most. But for some, a tiny number, the idea sticks. It keeps them up at night.

"And a tiny number of those people go out and do it. Murder. Some in the moment. Some plan it out. Doesn't matter. They all get caught."

"All of them?" said Gordon. "Can't be."

"All of them. And it's because they've all got the same problem once it's done. The victim. A big, dead receipt for your transaction. If there's a body, there's going to be an investigation. And no matter how careful you thought you were, there will be something that leads the investigators right to you."

Gordon thought for a minute. "So this garden, where we're headed, they deal with bodies?"

"Yes," said Chandler. "It's near impossible to prove there was a murder without a corpse. The Gladdoms make it go away."

"But couldn't they, the Gladdoms, use that against you? The remains, the evidence, I mean."

"I said they make it go away. Vanish. No evidence. Been doing this for centuries."

———

Moss and Buchannon arrived at Dorling CID. "You get a look at all the mad things they found at his place?" asked Buchannon.

"Nightmare stuff," said Moss. "They had to leave most of it. Wanted to make sure it wasn't, um, what did they call it? 'Volatile?'"

"This is monster movie stuff," said Buchannon, "Like in the pictures." They walked into Roger Weeks' office, as they had been instructed. Behind his desk, Weeks sorted through a mountain of forms.

"Hello, Boss," said Buchannon. "Has the doctor opened up yet?"

"We may never know," said Weeks.

"How do you mean?" asked DS Moss.

"He's been taken. Carted off to an undisclosed location. Everything we had in the evidence room has been taken as well. The house at Boulton Heath has been sealed up and we can't get near it."

"How?" asked Buchannon.

"They brought a dozen vans," said Weeks. He tapped the pile on his desk. "These are papers from the Home Secretary's Office. They thank us for our work thus far. We have been notified that this business is no longer our concern. They came out of nowhere and gave us the boot."

"Blimey," said Moss. "It's bloody MI5!"

"What about Raddison? Theodore Raddison, the one we found tied to the bed."

"Him?" said Weeks, "Got a call from my brother. He checked himself out hours ago. No one knows where he is."

XIII

By her face, most would guess Laurel Gladdom was in her eighties. Her deep voice might add a few years to the estimate. But once she started moving, her light steps and speed would send all previous guesses out the window.

She stood over a small trailer where Chandler and Gordon had just deposited Walt Lymon, wrapped in a tarp.

"Sour old bastard," she said. "Been seeing too much of him lately. Unpleasant fellow, he was. At least he'll be of some use now."

Her grandson, Reggie Gladdom, hooked the trailer to a short Massey Ferguson tractor. "Where to, Nanny?" he asked.

"Reggie, you've got to think clearer. Where were you digging earlier?"

Reggie chewed on this for a moment. "Lot six three nine. The mums."

"Right. That's where he's off to. But wait for Dean, eh?"

After a moment, Dean Gladdom, Reggie's older brother, came along with a wheelbarrow filled with supplies. Reggie was in his thirties but looked much younger. Dean, in his forties, looked younger than Reggie.

"Mr. Chandler!" said Dean. "Haven't seen you in a while."

"Hello Dean," said Chandler. "You're looking well. How's your parents?"

"Good as ever," said Dean. "Who's your friend?"

"This is Jerry Gordon. He's helping me today."

"Nice to meet you," said Gordon. "All of you."

Gordon had to keep his cover going. He was in the middle of a place where criminals got rid of bodies. Terrible place to announce you're a policeman.

"You seem a nice young man," said Laurel Gladdom.

"Thank you, Ma'am," said Gordon.

"Please," she said, "Call me Nanny. Everyone does. Come here and have a look at what Dean's got."

Gordon came over and watched Dean move the supplies to the trailer. "This is the mix, kid," said Nanny Gladdom. "Don't ever do it different. Been using this same mix for over a hundred years. Maybe longer. No one knows for sure."

Dean rattled off the inventory as he placed the items. "Once the goods are in a hole, four feet down, these get spread over them. Two buckets of lye, one of quicklime. Then, a bottle of wine. Then what do we do, Reggie?"

"Don't forget to fill the hole back in," said Reggie.

"It all works with the gas and heat from the mosses," said Chandler. "Come back in a week. There won't be anything here. Nothing you'd notice, anyway."

"Not you, not the raccoons or the wolves," said Nanny Gladdom. "And definitely not the fuzz. The flowers love it, though. All these worthless tossers finally get to be of some use. Best thing for these blooms."

"Dean, they've brought us a car," said Reggie.

"Really?" said Dean.

"It's a blue Vauxhall," said Chandler. "Your Nanny's got the papers."

"Can't wait to try it," said Dean.

"Work first," said Nanny Gladdom. "Go with your brother to six three nine and help him get this horrid twat into the hole. And don't forget to wear gloves. Who knows where he's been?"

Dean climbed on the tractor's fender behind Reggie, and they headed out along a path between the blooms.

"Well," said Nanny Gladdom, "let's go have a cuppa and wait for the boys to get back."

The Gladdom home was full of country charm. For all the dirt surrounding the place, there wasn't a speck inside.

They sat in a large kitchen. Nanny Gladdom placed a tray of home-made tea cakes in the middle of the table and put the kettle on to boil.

"Let me ask you, Pat," said Nanny Gladdom, "why had Walt been visiting so often?"

"Not sure I follow," said Chandler.

"He's been up here nearly once a week lately," she said. "And he's calling in the vans as well. He said these meths drinkers and junkies were causing trouble, sleeping rough near Mr. Barnes' more legitimate businesses. He said they passed around some bad stuff, started turning up dead. They must have been in an awful state. He had them wrapped up tight when they got here. Oh, there's the kettle."

She poured the water into the teapot and continued. "He said Mr. Barnes didn't want the coppers involved, so Walt brung them here. Stack of cash for four of them in the first lot. Then a week later he's got another. Used the van for that one. Then two more. On and on."

"This is news to me," said Chandler.

Reggie and Dean returned and made a rush for the teacakes. "Here!" said Nanny Gladdom. "Those are for company. And did you wash your hands?"

"Yes, Nanny," the boys chorused, showing their palms.

"All right then, one each, but at the table and on a plate, not wandering in your mitts like bloody apes."

"You've got me curious," said Chandler. "If these pour souls Walt brought you poisoned themselves with something, won't they hurt your flowers?"

"No," said Nanny Gladdom. "Been putting them all up in lot fourteen, lily of the valley. Those *are* poison, and you know—"

"I thought they was good for the gout," said Dean.

"I'll give you gout," said Nanny Gladdom. "And don't interrupt, you twat. It's rude. Anyway, they're poison, even though there's some who say it's medicine."

"That's what I heard," said Dean.

"Shut it. Like I said, those lilies of the valley are tough. They love acid and all kinds of terrible soil. Who knows what these creeps Walt brung me had inside them, so they all went to lot fourteen."

There wasn't much conversation on the way back to Dorling. The flatbed's radio kept Chandler and Gordon informed about the royal wedding happening tomorrow.

"They're nice, the Gladdoms," said Gordon.

"Yes," said Chandler.

"You all right, Mr. Chandler? Seems like you're a million miles away."

"Sorry, thinking is all. I just know those deliveries

Walt made were from that nut case out on Boulton Heath."

"I'm not sure I follow," said Gordon.

"Dangerous work out there. He wanted people who wouldn't be missed. Mad science stuff. Dexter made it clear he wanted nothing to do with it."

"And Walt went and did it, anyway? On his own?"

"Yeah. Hope this hasn't hurt the garden."

The flatbed returned to Dorling Tyre and Auto Repair. Pat Chandler headed out in his Aston Martin DBS to take care of whatever else was on his list.

Jerry Gordon said his goodbyes and drove off down Hainsley Road.

———

DI Buchannon's phone rang at Dorling CID. Graham Pierce was calling.

"Hello," said Buchannon, "it's good to hear your voice."

"Cheers, Mike," said Pierce. "A lot has happened since we talked this morning."

"True. We're checking into Prestige Motors. Good work."

"Thanks, but that's not important. You know the business you told me about? Out on Boulton Heath? Well, Walt and Nigel were supplying your crazy doctor with his victims, then using a flower farm out in The Fens to get rid of the remains."

"What?"

"There's more. Barnes knew what the doctor was up to and forbade his crew from doing anything with him. Walt and Nigel acted on their own."

"We've been looking for them. No luck."

"You won't find Walt," said Pierce. "He's pushing up daisies."

"Really?"

"Mums, actually. It's not important. Well, the flowers are important, and your involuntary nudists. I think I've cracked it. Can you arrest me?"

Buchannon pulled the phone away from his ear and looked at it. Returning it to his ear, he said, "Do what now?"

"I'm at a phone box a block from the garage. I need to come to the nick and check on something, but if I walk in, I'll blow my cover. So, get a car to The Ragged Lion and bring me in to help with your inquiries."

Twenty minutes later, Graham Pierce and Mike Buchannon were in a conference room at Dorling CID. Case files and back issues of the Sun were strewn about the table.

"It's right here in Bennett's report," said Buchannon. "The nude man left a trail of garments and his shopping, and a bunch of flowers were left in the gutter. Flowers, again."

"And here, more pictures in The Sun," said Pierce. "This happened at a flower market, see? And this one, there's a bouquet on the ground with their clothes."

"Moss and I witnessed this with some ladies in a café," said Buchannon. "Three of them and one had a bouquet. But whatever this is, it doesn't affect everyone. Otherwise, the whole place would have been a naked party."

"You told me that doctor messed about with people's brains," said Pierce. "Intelligence. Will. Freedom. Whatever he put in those poor people, it also got into their remains. And then into the flowers. And with some people, just some, the scent of those flowers makes them giddy. Makes them want to jump around without clothes."

"See if you can find anything else in these files," said Buchannon. "I'm going to make a call."

Eight minutes later, Buchannon came back. "Pierce," he said, "You're coming with me. We're headed to The Fens."

Graham Pierce looked confused.

"Yes, they know me, and I know them," said Buchannon. "Honestly, did you think criminals were the only ones who need to get rid of a body now and then?"

XIV

When Graham Pierce and Mike Buchannon got to Gladdom's Bloom Farm, they found Nanny Gladdom and Dean sitting on the porch with Reggie, wrapped up in a blanket.

Smiling.

"It's just like you said on the phone, Mike," said Nanny Gladdom.

"Yeah," said Dean. "Reggie and I went up to lot fourteen and popped open a couple of buds on those lily of the valley. All of the sudden, Reggie gets naked and starts dancing around."

"And not the way he usually does," said Nanny Gladdom. "This were a lot more graceful. And Dean here wasn't affected at all." She noticed Pierce. "Oh, you're back Mr. Gordon."

"I guess I should explain," said Pierce.

"Bollocks," said Nanny Gladdom. "I thought you looked like a copper. Well, no matter. We're all working the same job now."

"You know," said Dean, "running around, all natural-like, it kind of sounds wonderful. Free, you know?"

"Well sod off and go be free and naked, then," said Nanny Gladdom. "In the meantime, the rest of us have got to figure out where those damn flowers have gone before some poor dear drops their trousers at Charing Cross and dances in front of a train."

———

Edric and Andrea Gladdom were Reggie and Dean's parents. They ran the main shop in London. There, all the records of sales and travel were kept. Over the next two hours, they hunted down every bunch of lily of the valley in their stores and elsewhere.

Mike Buchannon and Graham Pierce came through the door just as Nanny Gladdom hung up the phone. They had been helping Dean burn out lot fourteen and they were filthy.

"Well," said Buchannon, "where do we stand?"

Nanny Gladdom closed her logbook and rubbed her eyes. "Good thing we keep tight on the books and the forms," she said. "We've cleared the lily of the valley out of the shops and pulled the orders back in. They're going in the incinerators now. We told them it was a bug problem, orders from the Ministry of Agriculture."

"Great," said Pierce. "It's all sorted then."

"No." said Nanny Gladdom. "No, it isn't, not by a far sight. There's still one big bouquet out there with those lily of the valley in it. Went out special from our London shop this morning. And these customers won't fall for some twaddle about bugs."

"Well, let's pick it up," said Dean. "Who is this customer?"

"The Queen," said Nanny Gladdom. "It's Anne's bouquet. Princess Anne. She'll be carrying those crazy makers down the aisle at Westminster tomorrow."

"Oh, no," said Buchannon. "If she's one of the ones that's susceptible...and everything is going out live on telly!"

"All over the world," said Pierce. "With the bride in her starkers."

"It won't stop with her. Anyone around might be affected. What if the Queen herself comes close? 'You look lovely, dear. Oh, let me smell those flowers, they're just beautiful!' And the royal garments drop and the monarch twirls about in the altogether."

The room fell silent. Partly because the scenario described was horrible. And partly because the words were spoken by Pat Chandler.

"Hello Pat," said Buchannon.

"Hello Mike," said Chandler.

"You know each other?" asked Pierce.

"We were both in the Muller Houses," said Buchannon. "We went our separate ways."

"Time to come together," said Chandler. "We've got work to do. For the sake of the country, for the Crown, we must get those flowers."

"Yes," said Buchannon.

"We need to a plan," said Nanny Gladdom. "Go wash up. I've got some pork pies ready to go in the oven. Just the thing for planning."

———

"I wondered when you'd call," said Nigel. He was in a hotel in South London.

"Wonder no longer," said the voice on the line. "Heard about Walt going missing. Hope he's all right."

"Oh, he's missing all right. But he's not all right. He's missing for good. Gone to the garden, I heard."

"There will be an investigation," said the voice. "Is there anything to connect me with any of this nonsense?"

"No," said Nigel. "Nothing is written down, and you were never at the scene. No prints, no nothing."

"Good," said the voice. "You know, the coppers combed through the doc's place like a line of hungry ants. Then MI5 took everything the coppers had in evidence and they shook down Boulton Heath all over again."

"I can't imagine we can get anything for your buyer, then."

"Not so fast. It turns out there's a trace of the doctor's work nobody knew about. It's in London, and we may be able to get our hands on it. Won't be easy, though."

"What do you mean 'trace?'" asked Nigel.

"Something I overheard. A whiff of the mind-essence has found its way into some flowers."

"How does that work?"

"I don't know how it works. What's more, I don't have to. What I do know is there's a bunch of flowers with a bit of that brain sauce in their buds. The buyer will want it."

"All right," said Nigel. "But what makes this bunch of flowers so hard to get hold of?"

"Well, it's quite a story…"

XV

DI Mike Buchannon arrived at Westminster Abbey in one of the vans from Dorling CID, just like the rest of the officers. They checked in and took their positions, some working the crowds, some helping with traffic. The ceremony was hours off, but the streets were already mad with onlookers.

Gladdom's Blooms had a legitimate entry on the vendor list. They were bringing bunches of white roses to decorate the walkways and photo areas. Four people were in the Gladdom's van: Dean Gladdom, Patrick Chandler, Jerry Gordon, and Lionel Barris.

The rose arrangements were already put together, stacked in special cases. One of those cases also held a sealed black box with an exact copy of Princess Anne's bouquet. Without the dangerous buds, of course.

The guard at the main entrance checked them off and let them through. The Gladdom's van rolled in with Dean Gladdom driving.

Getting inside the building would be the tricky bit.

The four men piled out, looking smart in their Gladdom's Blooms delivery togs, but Chandler's looked a little tight.

"Right," said Chandler. "Stay together and remember, Dean is in charge." He looked around. "Christ, where's Lionel gone?"

"I'm right here," said Lionel.

"Oh, very good. All right, Dean. Lead the way."

Dean brought them to the back of the van, and each man took two cases of flowers stacked one on top of the other, reaching just under their chins. Dean closed up the van with a well-practiced kick.

The foursome moved through a vendor circus behind the Abbey. Photographers, caterers, sommeliers, lighting technicians, all trying to figure out where they were supposed to be and how to best get there.

Lionel looked to the queue at the main door.

"There's our way in. Copper checking credentials looks serious. Is he with us?"

"No, he's not," said Pierce.

It was Constable Maurice Pixley. He had a clipboard with names and expectations.

The Gladdom's group joined the queue. The list had Dean Gladdom's name, but the other three wouldn't match. No Barris. No Chandler. No Gordon.

Or Pierce. He kept his head down and hat pulled low, just in case Pixley recognized him through the beard and dark hair.

They were up next. Pixley clicked his pen twice. "Hello, and who are we with?"

"Gladdom's Blooms," said Dean, turning to show the logo on the back of his togs.

"Yes, and what are you doing here this morning?"

Dean held up his cases. "We are placing these roses around the walkways and photo areas. Dressing the place, you know."

"Roses, eh? I see. Your name?"

"Dean. Dean Gladdom."

"Ah. Like in 'Gladdom's Blooms,'" said Pixley, flipping pages on his clipboard. "There you are— Dean Gladdom. May I see your driving license or passport?"

A rolling baritone interrupted. "Constable Pixley? A moment, please."

"Oh, good morning DCI Weeks. Let me just finish—"

Roger Weeks engaged *the voice*. "Now, Pixley. Let those people with the flowers through. You lot, behind them, hang on just a minute, please."

Pixley stepped away and answered Weeks' questions about today's schedule.

The men from Gladdom's Blooms were in.

They walked in a straight line until Dean found

someone with a broom. People with brooms know everything. "Excuse me," he said. "We're a bit turned around. Where is the walk-in fridge where they are keeping the flowers?"

"Just down that hall," said the woman with the broom. "Two rights, can't miss it."

"Thank you." The group moved in that direction and stopped for a meeting after the first turn.

"So far, so good," said Chandler. "Lionel, time for you to get...where's Lionel?"

This time, he wasn't there.

"Lionel?" said Gordon. "He's not here. He's carried off his crates and vanished."

"And he's got the proper bouquet," said Dean.

"Let's head for the fridge," said Chandler. "Maybe we'll find him along the way."

They went down the hall. They took the next right. They found the fridge, just where the woman with the broom said it would be.

"Great," said Dean. "Here's the fridge, but where's Lionel?"

"I'm right here," said Lionel.

There he stood, both crates of roses up to his chin.

"Christ, Lionel," said Chandler. "We've got to figure out how we're going to get you in there to swap those flowers."

"But I already done it. They're swapped."

Silence.

"It's not locked," said Lionel. "It's a church. They don't lock nothing."

"Any danger of us getting a whiff of those crazy fumes?" asked Chandler.

Dean checked the box. "No," he said. "Totally sealed. Keeps the flowers fresh."

"Well, let's get out of here," said Lionel.

"Can't," said Dean. "We still have to do the job

we're here for. My job, setting these roses up. Queen and Country are one thing, but Gladdom's is getting a lot of money for this."

They spent half an hour under Dean's direction. The walkways and photo areas looked lovely when they were finished.

"Now we can leave," said Dean.

Getting out of the building was easier than getting in. They walked out the door and casually toward the van. Halfway there, DI Mike Buchannon joined up and walked with them. "Any trouble?" he asked.

"Got the goods," said Chandler. "Still have to roll out, but I think it's going to be all right."

Dean opened the back of the van, and everyone loaded in their cases, using extra caution with Lionel's. With all the trouble stowed away, the group shared a deep breath.

"That was fun," said Lionel.

"Well done, all," said Buchannon. He and Chandler shook hands.

Dean rubbed his neck. "I'm knackered," he said. "Someone else should drive."

Pierce moved up front to the van's door. He found the seat occupied.

"Sorry, mate. My turn to drive." Nigel Wilkes swung the door hard and knocked Pierce to the ground. He started the engine, and the van rolled toward the exit.

"What's he doing here?" asked Chandler.

"He must want the flowers," said Pierce.

A uniformed officer appeared and stood defiantly in front of the van, blocking the way. "Blimey!" said Buchannon. "That's Pixley! Who knew? He's a hero!"

Nigel stopped and Constable Maurice Pixley jumped into the passenger seat, smiling.

"Oh," said Buchannon. "He's not a hero. He's a prick. A bloody accomplice."

Everyone ran toward the van, but there was no way they'd reach it. Pierce waved his hands over his head and pointed at the escaping vehicle.

A pair of workers carrying a tall ladder nodded to Pierce. They crossed in front of the van and stopped moving. Nigel had to hit the brakes. He put it in reverse, only to have that way blocked by another set of workers with another ladder.

Nigel rolled down his window. "Get out of the way!"

More workers with more ladders surrounded the van. They cut the valve stems on the tyres. This escape vehicle wasn't going anywhere. It had been surrounded by a group that was all racket, piss, and chaos.

Pixley grabbed the box of flowers. He and Nigel scrambled out of their disabled get-away van, only to be trapped in a hastily formed cage made of ladders.

"Oi," called Martin Reynolds. "Where do you want these twits?"

"The Divers Hands just earned a year's worth of wages," said Chandler.

From nowhere, a black town car without plates rolled in. Three agents emerged, brushing The Hands aside. Two of them put handcuffs on Nigel and Pixley and moved the pair of them, plus the flowers, into the town car. A third agent presented a form to DI Buchannon. Then, with a tiny bow, he returned to the car as well.

Everyone gathered around Buchannon. "What's it say?" asked Chandler.

"It's our friends from the Home Secretary's Office again. They've taken the buds and the conspirators. They thank us for our assistance."

Lionel laughed. "Doesn't really matter, does it? I'm going to the nearest pub and watch the wedding on telly. Anyone want to come along?"

Everyone wanted to come along.

Graham Pierce and Pat Chandler were looking at each other, wondering who would be the first to speak.

Pat Chandler smiled. "You do good work, Jerry Gordon. I won't hold the fact that you're a copper against you."

"Remember," said Buchannon, "it's not Gordon, it's Pierce. Detective Sergeant Graham Pierce."

"Sorry, you've both got it wrong. My name isn't Jerry Gordon *or* Graham Pierce. My name is Henry Elgan, and I've been working deep cover for MI5. We thank you for everything you've done."

Henry Elgan stepped away from the group and climbed into the town car. They rolled off, and he wasn't seen again.

Buchannon looked at Dean. "What does this mean for you? For Gladdom's Bloom Farm? That man, Elgan, he knows everything!"

"For us?" said Dean. "Nothing. MI5, MI6, all of them have been doing business with Gladdoms for ages. Now let's get to that pub."

Trivia

Murder Garden ran in theaters on both sides of the Atlantic during the spring of 1974. It was adapted from a novella of the same name, reprinted here.

This was the first of three World Cinema Group coproductions with the Rank Organisation. It was followed by the erotic horror film *Satan's Satin Angels*. Next came the werewolf thriller *Moonlit Oblivion*.

Location shooting in The Fens lasted only two days, with the cast and crew lodging at the South Angle Farm, which served as the Gladdom's Bloom Farm in the film.

This film was actor Clive Dearing's feature debut. To make it a greater challenge, he played three roles: Constable Pixley, Doctor Marchworth, and Nanny Gladdom. All were based on characters he created for his music hall performances. It's the reason these characters don't share any scenes in the film.

Ten years after this film's release, director Lance Holden revealed mob ties of his own, as his massive gambling debts forced him into bankruptcy.

Filming at Westminster Abbey was forbidden, so they used stock footage for the exteriors and Liverpool Cathedral for the interiors.

The "mix" used at Gladdom's to make the buried corpses vanish was a complete fabrication of the writer. Indeed, several experts have noted that the steps shown in the film would likely preserve a body, rather than dispose of one.

Lighting assistant Roger Messing was a long-distance runner and quite thin. Because of his light weight (130 pounds), he portrayed every corpse that was carried on camera.

Prehistoric impossibilities walk again to KILL KILL KILL! From the far-off mire they came, now they are here to FEAST! Will you survive the slime-drenched terror? Can anything defeat ... THE BOG FIENDS!

Turn this book over for
second complete novel

BOG FIENDS

BRET NELSON

Encyclopocalypse Publications
www.encyclopocalypse.com

Foreword

The first time I met Harold J. Kerr, it was in a little sweatbox cutting room at his offices on Gower Street in Hollywood. It was the spring of 1970, and a friend had recommended me as an editor.

Mind you, at that time, I had only cut news footage for a local TV station. But at 23-years-old, I was available and cheap, so I got the interview.

His offices covered the third floor of the building. To get in, you had to hold your thumb against a filthy button and wait for someone to answer the intercom. It had a crappy speaker, and you could hardly understand what was being said, but it was always Harry's voice. And it always ended with the buzzer drowning out him as he shouted for you to hurry through the door.

He didn't care about my lack of experience. He said, "If you know how to use the gear, Tony will show you the rest." He was talking about Anthony Wrigley, who was hunched over a Moviola and trying hard to ignore us. Wrigley was deep into his 60s at this time and had a pile of credits going all the way back to the Depression.

The three of us spent the rest of the day in that

tiny room, squinting at an Italian sword and sandals film that Kerr just got the rights to. I can't remember the title.

(It was *"Il terrore dei esercito fantasma,"* 1968 from Produzioni Giganti – Ed.)

He was going to dub and distribute the picture, but that's not why we were cutting it. He wanted to extract the huge battle sequences so they could stand alone. Just the big shots with the ancient armies. That way, he could use the footage to pad out cheap period scripts.

This one acquisition would become two or three other movies.

"In the Shakespeare plays," he said, "the battles happen offstage, but the play happens in the rooms of the castle. That's what I'll do. Shoot the human drama in the castle then cut to these great fight scenes happening outside."

By the end of that day, I had lost 5 pounds due to sweat, and learned everything I would ever need to know about editing. And Harold J. Kerr had the fight scenes that would become the guts of *Titan meets the Vampire Death Force (1971)* and *Hercules versus the Two-Headed Caligula (1973)*.

They weren't at all like Shakespeare.

I was told to come back the following Monday at 7:30am.

I showed up as instructed, went up the stairs three floors (there was an elevator, but I don't recall if it ever worked), and Harry led me to an even smaller cutting room with an even older splicing setup. There were a dozen film cans stacked up and a thick binder (screenplay with director/script supervisor notes) on top. And I started cutting *Bog Fiends*.

Title card for Bog Fiends (1969)

There wasn't any kind of negotiation for pay. He just asked me what I was making at the TV station, said "I can't afford that," and wrote me a check for less. "That will cover your first week, then we'll see if you get another one," he said. And just like that, I was expected to deliver *Bog Fiends* in five days.

I completely lucked out. The director, Teddy Barrett, shot very lean. He was an old pro and the whole picture was easier to put together than a lot of the news stories I'd done. I was a pain in Wrigley's neck when it came to getting the music and sound effects in, but even that process wasn't as daunting as I thought it would be.

And a decent bottle of gin would right any wrong with Wrigley.

I was with World Cinema Group for the next five years, off and on. It's nice to see *Bog Fiends* getting some attention. I thought it was a good little movie.

Don't get me started on that two-headed Roman pervert picture, though. The fact that it's a "lost film" is the only good thing about it.

Jerry Thorinson, (June, 2022)
Past President, Motion Pictures Editors Guild

BOG FIENDS

It's over now.

It's over, and the doctors told me I've healed enough to use a typewriter again. I'm not even sure *The Globe* will run this. It's not the story they hired me to write. If they do print it, the moon landing will push this to the newspaper's back pages, anyway.

When I signed their contract back in March, I thought this would be my best year. I thought I'd be writing a story about success. About how progress can benefit society. But no one knew what was coming. No one could have guessed what waited deep in that bog.

Now, it's become a story about a man who had the means to realize his greatest dream, and the fiends who tore that dream to pieces.

———

Last Spring, the entire country was talking about Malcolm Lerner, the wealthiest man in the world. He was working on something huge, even for him, but he kept the project secret. Every paper coast to coast (and many overseas) ran a headline claiming to have the scoop:

"Malcolm Lerner to announce candidacy for President," — *The Times*

"Billionaire set to reveal plans for international jet transit hub," — *Tribune Publications*

"Manufacturing giant readies 'city-sized' factory," — *The Journal*

And they all had it wrong. Lerner wrote the kind of checks that bought absolute secrecy.

I'd been working steadily, but I hadn't had an assignment with teeth for months. Then, late on a Tuesday night, I got a call from one of my favorite editors. We both got our start in Chicago decades ago. Now she ran *The Globe*, a national paper headquartered in San Francisco.

"Tony? Tony Rogers? It's Marla Benford."

"Marla?" I asked. It was a lousy connection. "Marla—like, from Chicago?"

"Yes, that one. Really Tony, how many Marla's are there? Tell me, what are you working on right now and how much cash do I need to get you out of it?"

Something in her voice compelled you to answer each of her questions succinctly. "I'm at *The Herald*. Right now, I'm finishing up a facts and figures story on that new movie from Sterling Productions. Most expensive comedy in history and everybody wants it to flop. Handing it in on Thursday then getting my next assignment."

"Are you under contract and can I buy you out of it?"

"No contract. I am free to leave after this gets turned in, but I'll burn a bridge if I just duck out."

I heard a lighter spark. She'd started smoking again, and that meant something big in the works. She puffed out slowly and gave me her pitch.

"I need you to come to San Francisco, to *The Globe*," she said. "We've got the exclusive on Malcolm Lerner's secret project. He wants one reporter to follow him around for the next year, while they get the whole thing up and running. I get to pick the reporter, and I pick you."

"How many..."

"I've got three names on my list, but I called you first. It's a good thing you haven't changed your number. It's a good thing you answered the phone."

I waited a few seconds so as not to sound eager. "Okay. I'm still listening."

"The assignment is for the whole year," said Marla. "That's twelve months shadowing Lerner. You'll send brief update articles from the field, but you're really working on a bigger piece. At the end, we'll do a double truck special every day for the week leading up to the opening. Those are all you. Then, we'll run a full color section on the opening Sunday, lots of pages. That's you as well. We've even got a book deal pre-sold."

"How did you convince him,—oh wait, Lerner owns *The Globe*, doesn't he? No convincing needed. So why me? Don't you have an army of staffers who can fluff and softball your boss for a year?"

"It's not what he wants," said Marla. "He needs the public to buy in. Says this one thing is his big legacy. He wants an objective reporter who can find cracks in his plan, one who can dive all the way down."

"Can you tell me what it is?" I asked. "This big legacy thing?"

"Not until you sign. I can have your contract all written up and ready for Monday. Just tell me what you want to be paid."

———

Well, I had to say "yes," didn't I?

My exit from *The Herald* was uncomplicated. The managing editor wished me well, but he got my name wrong. Called me "Robert." I hope the real Robert didn't have trouble getting new assignments.

The following Monday at the Globe Building in San Francisco, I signed my life away with non-disclosure, proprietary information, and confidentiality

agreements. The portion of the contracts dealing with my writing and pay were only ten pages out of one hundred and fifty.

Once the lawyers were finished with me, I was alone in the conference room, wondering what came next. "Be with you in a sec," said a voice. A petite brunette sat by the window, finishing some notes. Earlier, the attorneys at the conference table monopolized my field of view, so I hadn't seen her.

She looked younger than any of the lawyers by half. I figured her for an intern. "Excuse me," I said. "Don't you have to help them get back into their coffins?"

She didn't look up. "Not until sunrise," she said. "I'm free until then."

She finished her notes, then glided over to me with her hand extended. "Hello Anthony Rogers, I'm Theresa Meddings, but please call me Terry."

We shook hands. As our eyes met, it felt like she looked deep inside me, right into the place where I kept all my secrets. She was welcome there.

Those were rare eyes.

"It's a pleasure, Terry," I said. "Call me Tony."

"All right, Tony. Let's talk while we walk. This way, please." We left the conference room and sailed through the hallways of the 37th floor. Her steps were quick and light. Her turns sharp and confident. I could barely keep up.

"Now that our paper army has had their way with you, we can talk freely," she said. "I'm going to take you down to the site. There, you'll be introduced to Mr. Lerner. Don't be intimidated. He's hired you to share everything you see and hear with everyone in the world. You'll find he's quite candid."

"What do you—"

"Mr. Lerner has set up systems to maximize his time. I lead his advance team. We move in front of him, making certain the next thing is ready for him before he gets there. Right now, I have people working on jobs he won't touch for another six months. He steps off the cliff and onto our bridge just as we've completed it. Full efficiency."

"I covered a trapeze family once. Sounds like that."

"If they were responsible for seventeen billion dollars in assets and over two hundred thousand jobs worldwide, then yes, it's like that. Into the elevator, please."

She didn't brief me on the mystery project. Malcolm Lerner wanted to do it. The elevator took us to the roof, where a helicopter waited. The chopper took us to San Francisco International Airport, where a Lockheed Jetstar waited. The jet took us to Lindbergh Field in San Diego. That's what she meant by "down" to the site.

Terry said I should use the travel time to sort out my questions for Lerner. I soon learned everyone in the organization used travel time for working. There were six other people on the plane, all involved in a prep meeting with Terry. They were getting together with Lerner in the afternoon to discuss an issue with his ball bearing plants in Europe.

During our short flight, Terry helped them prune their twelve-page agenda down to three questions. And two of those were "yes or no."

There were a pair of limousines waiting at Lindbergh. The bearing people got into one and I never saw them again. Terry and I headed for the other. Our driver, Bart Charles, had been with Lerner for fifteen years. The bulge in his jacket told me he had a

shoulder holster, making him private security and wheelman.

He opened the back door of the limo and we climbed in. Emilia Berrington, one of my favorite photographers, was already in the car. Her shots always told a complete story, and you never even knew she was there. Our paths first crossed in Korea, seems like ages ago now. I was one of four war correspondents working for *The Chicago Star*, with Marla as our managing editor. Emilia also worked for the *Star*, but not as support for my stories. She shot her own photo essays, and they were amazing. Since then, she'd mainly been working for the glossies.

"I don't think I need to introduce you two," said Terry.

"No, you don't," said Emilia. "Where's my twenty bucks, Rogers?"

"They aren't on the moon yet," I said. "People on the moon before the end of the decade, that's the bet. On the moon. They still aren't there."

"It's all right. I can wait. Looks like we're going to be busy until then, anyway. I was glad when Marla told me you were the writer on this."

"It's good to see you, too. Are you just starting?"

"I got here like ten minutes ago," said Emilia. "It's my first day."

"So, you don't know what we're covering, either."

"You each have the same amount of information, which isn't much," said Terry. "However, within the next three hours, you'll know everything." She tapped on the glass panel behind Bart's head, and we rolled out.

———

When you see California on television, you think it's all developed. Every show takes place in San Francisco, Los Angeles, or the suburbs. In reality, only a tiny portion of the state has grown into cities, while the rest has been unchanged since the rivers pulled back to expose the land millions of years ago.

We were headed to the swamps. As you move south, the postcard beaches and movie-star surfers fade away. The water and the land come together to form bogs and marshes just like you'd find along the same latitude in Louisiana or Florida.

Over the next two hours, the limo moved off the highway, then off the main road, then onto a gravel road. The suspension and tires were customized to handle the rough terrain. No sign of people as far as you could see.

No sign of anything, not even a power line or passing aircraft. Our gravel path was on sturdy ground, but we were surrounded by marshes and ponds. Emilia's Pentax clicked constantly. She already snapped dozens of shots of the nothing surrounding us.

Finally, we reached the end of the road, where the gravel and dry land stopped with only marsh beyond. An aluminum launch and a swamp boat sat in the water, tied off to the bumper of a parked jeep. A military tent big enough to house ten people stood nearby.

"We're here," said Bart, parking behind the jeep.

We got out of the limo and Terry went into the tent, instructing us to stand by. Emilia and I got a closer look at the swamp boat. "These are the loudest things on Earth," she said. "Ever been in one?"

"Yes, covering those floods outside of Jacksonville a couple of years ago. It smelled just like this place, sharp. Reaches all the way behind your eyes."

"Yeah, I'm getting that." She called to Bart. "Hey handsome, you got any mosquito repellent on board?" He trotted to the trunk, then over to us with an orange aerosol can.

"Deet, high concentration," he said. "It's the best. Hit everything with it, even your hair and your shoes." Emilia and I created a fog bank of the stuff.

"Thanks, you're my hero," said Emilia, tossing the can back to Bart. "I thought a super-secret rich-guy project would be more impressive. This looks like a moonshine camp. Is there a still in the tent?"

"I wouldn't know, ma'am." said Bart.

Terry popped out of the tent and held the flap open. Malcolm Lerner stepped out to greet us.

Lerner was my age, which made me realize how little I'd accomplished given an equal number of years. No pricey suit. The man didn't even wear a tie, though his linen shirt was neatly pressed. The jeans were brand new. Short, brown hair and a clean shave.

He charged at me. "There he is! Hello, Tony!" He shook my hand with three fierce tugs. "Terry said I should call you 'Tony,' hope that's all right. Do you know how to ride a motorcycle?"

"Uh, no," I said. "I mean, I've done it, but I'm lousy at it. Cars and boats are all..."

"Boats! Useful skill. Good. Shame about the motorcycles, though. You'll have to learn. It's the best way to get around out here, the best way. Ah! Miss Berrington!" Emilia got the run-at-you-handshake-treatment.

"Your pictures of those volunteers working at the polling places in Arkansas—amazing," he said.

"Uh…thanks." She never knew what to do with a compliment.

Terry called from the tent. "Let's step inside, please."

A portable air conditioner made the interior of the tent cool and dry. It looked like the bullpen of an office building. There were three people seated at a conference table strewn with aerial images and schematics.

"This," said Terry, indicating the man sketching at the conference table, "is Ian Dorney, our chief architect."

"Hello," he said. Dorney spoke quietly. He might have been shy about his brogue. A big man with rough edges, born and raised in Cliara, Ireland. He studied architecture at Oxford and Berkeley. If I had been asked to guess his profession, I would have gone with blacksmith.

"And this is Doctor Alex Rankin," said Terry, moving around the table, "and his assistant, Jerry Thompson." Jerry had trouble making eye contact. I could tell he had spent most of his time in school. This job was likely his first.

Rankin looked every bit the scientist. Thin, almost unwell, with thick glasses covering most of his face. He and Jerry studied a spreadsheet. "Nice to meet you," said Rankin, without looking up. Jerry gave an awkward nod.

Terry led me to the table. "Tony, you're in this seat. Emilia, I'm guessing you want to wander and shoot."

"Hell yes."

Terry sat next to me. On the table, in front of my chair, I found a legal pad, three Dixon Ticonderoga pencils, and a Parker T-1 ballpoint pen.

I was in love.

"Malcolm, it's your room," said Terry.

"Thanks," said Lerner. He paced as he talked. "Okay, Tony and Emilia, hello and welcome. I apologize in advance to everyone who isn't Tony or Emilia because you already know most of this, but I still

wanted you all here. Anyway, out in the middle of nowhere, we are going to build the best place on the planet to live. A city. The ultimate city, designed to make people's lives better."

He pointed out marks on the aerial photographs. "We're here in this circle, and these lines mark the total area we've purchased." It had to be over fifty square miles.

"We're going to kick out the current residents, the frogs and mosquitos, then we are going to build a wonderful place." He flipped through a series of large schematic drawings. Neighborhoods, buildings, parks, all the pieces that make a city.

Lerner continued. "*Primo.* Our city's name is Primo. I heard a rumor about me going into government, but they're wrong. I don't want to fix what's broken. I want to start with nothing and build it right in the first place. We've spent five years..."

"Seven," said Terry.

"...seven years planning. Now we're starting work. In three months, we'll announce the plan to the public, then we'll make the world a better place to live. Come and see! Everybody out! Tony, bring your writing things. Come on!"

Outside, Bart waited with life vests. He helped everyone onto the launch, then took the rearmost seat and pulled the rope on the outboard motor. "Mr. Lerner, we're going on the main route, yes?"

"Absolutely, Bart. Right along Pacific Avenue." Slowly, with Bart on the tiller, the launch took us away from the tent.

Emilia feigned disappointment. "Oh, we don't get to go on the swamp boat?"

"That goofy thing is getting sent back," said Lerner. "Hard to steer. And way too loud."

Dorney brought his sketchbook and kept drawing.

Rankin and Jerry were sorting objects in a large plastic case. Terry had her eyes closed and chin up, enjoying the sun. She listened as Lerner talked and filled in anything he missed.

"I'm obsessed with planning," Lerner said. "My companies beat every competitor because we plan for ages before we spend real money. Our factory schematics take years to complete, but once they're up and running, we save millions of dollars annually because our focus is on efficient work and fatigue prevention." We passed an inflatable raft holding a plywood sign reading: "PRIMO: CITY LIMIT."

"We even count the number of steps to and from water coolers, bathrooms, and wastepaper baskets." Around the next hill, we were on Pacific Avenue.

Well, it would be Pacific Avenue one day. Now, it was a wide blue ribbon stretched between buoys that rocked as our launch went by. Lerner had used a combination of buoys, rafts, and pontoon structures to support signs and plywood facades. Together, they represented a half-mile section of the city laid out in actual scale. "We're taking everything we know and aiming it at civil engineering and urban planning. This is going to be my legacy. It looks a little rough now..."

"A little? It's embarrassing," said Dorney, the architect.

"Mr. Dorney's plans are exquisite," said Terry. "The lines of the buildings and the contours in the street will complement the scenic views. Even the colors are being tuned to the natural lighting at different times of the day and year."

"Everything will always look good," said Dorney. "Except now. Now it looks like an army surplus flea market rubbish heap."

"It will get there, Ian," said Lerner. "This time next

year, we'll be walking down this street and your library, right there, will take everyone's breath away." For the moment, a buoy holding up a sign reading "LIBRARY," marked the location. A seagull sat on top.

Lerner turned back to us. "This land, in and around the San Elijo Lagoon, you might think it's a terrible place to build, but it's actually ideal."

"And cheap, I bet," said Emilia.

"A frugal purchase, yes. Almost all the parcels were owned by a cross section of state and city departments. Been sitting on them for over a century. Nobody wanted them. And here we come with a cash offer for the whole thing, one buyer—one check."

Bart had to stop the boat for a moment. We were blocked by a patch of rotting marsh grass. He used an oar to clear the smelly mess. Then he turned the boat off Pacific Avenue and onto Summer Glade Circle. He held his left arm out, signaling the turn. No one saw it but me. We shared a laugh.

Lerner continued. "City Hall is that big sign, and the circle of green ribbon is the park. This part of the purchase was a little complicated. Big parcel, and the only one with a private owner. It's Walker Halloran, of Halloran Family Farms. If you've ever had an almond, you probably had one of his. Back in 1932, he wanted to try growing rice, so he bought this land for next to nothing. It didn't work out and he couldn't find another buyer. But the taxes were pennies, so he just sat on it. Now, sixty years later, he held out on me until he made his money back many times over."

Doctor Rankin finally spoke. "Can we stop here, please?" Bart killed the engine and used an oar to keep the launch from drifting. Rankin gathered samples of reeds and water, handing them to Jerry, who stored them in the case.

"The doctor is working with us on the ecology of the place," said Lerner.

"Please," said Rankin, "don't make me sound like a hippy." He traded PH strips with Jerry. "There are plants, insects, animals, and molds far more suited to this place than we humans. They've been here forever and have adapted perfectly."

"And they didn't have to cut a deal with the almond guy," said Emilia.

"Indeed. I am trying to find simple ways to add our species to the existing ecosystem without shocking either of them."

Jerry took over. "Yes, like, for instance, the mosquitos aren't as bad here as they are on the shore. We've been working with some pumping technology to keep the water moving, so the little bastards can't breed." He waited for a laugh. It never came, so he returned to cataloguing the PH values.

"'Little bastard' is the scientific term for 'mosquito,'" said Lerner. "Our lead engineer, Cyril Matheson, you'll meet him later. Anyway, he's ready to start the infrastructure for Phase One. Terry? Have I got it right?"

"Phase One. You're doing great," she may have been asleep.

"Okay. Over the next month or so, we'll clear most of this foliage out, then the dredgers will come in. Next comes water, gas, and electric. But look around, we don't have to drill or dig! It's so simple, we just sink the culverts, pipe, and conduit and support it with pilings. Then we drain and fill around it."

"Don't forget the good part," said Dorney.

"Tell them about the good part, Malcolm," said Terry.

"Oh," said Lerner. "We own all the utilities. We've

patented the dredging and construction processes used to build them, so we can sell them to other cities. And if Primo is successful, we've already purchased enough land in Texas to build another one. Only bigger."

"That *is* good," said Emilia.

"We're approaching Central," said Bart. Ahead, past some willow trees, we saw the concrete island they called *Central*, the first permanent piece of the City of Primo and our home base for the near future. The area where we left the limo and boarded the launch was called *City Limits.*

The island, as large as two football fields, was dotted with aluminum structures where forty people lived and worked. Several smaller islands were connected to Central via a series of pontoon bridges and docks. And just like Lerner said, people used motorcycles to get around.

Bart tied off the launch and made sure everyone got safely onto the island. Terry escorted Emilia to her quarters on the far side. Bart pointed to a fifteen-foot square shed.

"This one's you. Should be unlocked," he said.

Inside, it looked nicer than a lot of the hotel suites I've stayed in.

The largest structure on Central, an airplane hangar, covered most of the west end of the island. There wasn't room inside for even one plane, though, because everyone worked in this shared space.

Each department had its own work area in the hangar, identified by a banner hanging from the high ceiling. A fifteen-foot-wide scale model of the City of Primo occupied the middle of the space. I'd seen architectural models before, but nothing like this. Ian Dorney's work, his attention to detail, was remarkable. It looked like they had shrunk a real place.

In the farthest corner of the hangar, they built a free-standing lab and darkroom for Emilia. She put a sign by the red light over her door:

Keep out when the red light is on. Or off.

Twice daily, she made sure Bart was aware the sign didn't apply to him.

Telephone service didn't reach out here, so communication around the site worked through walkie talkies. If you needed to address a crowd, there were bullhorns. A radio in the hangar could get patched to a phone number, but Terry and Lerner monopolized it. Standing near the hanger, the radio's antenna reached seventy feet into the air, supported by a network of cabling.

The east end of the island held the generators, water tanks, and pumping stations that kept Central operational. The rest of the buildings surrounded a courtyard with picnic tables and shuffleboard courts.

The aluminum structures were different sizes, mostly for housing, but some served other functions. The mess hall fed all the island's residents three times a day. Chef Camille LaPierre made some of the best food I'd ever eaten. A guard house stood nearest the hanger, staffed by Bart and his two associates, Angela Jones and Gerald Ricci, both poached from Lerner's travel detail. In the next building, Dolores Carn, a retired army medic, was absolutely in charge of the two-bed hospital.

She's why I'm not dead.

———

For the first week, we spent little time at Central. We traveled with Lerner as he completed the last few deals to make his dream a reality. New York, Florida, Chicago, a different city every morning. I thought

we'd slow down when we got back to California, but in a single day we had business in San Francisco, then a meeting in the San Joaquin Valley, and then back to the Primo site.

An odd thing happens when you travel with a billionaire—you become a billionaire. I don't mean my bank balance jumped to ten figures, but I lived like it did. We never waited in a line. We always got the best everyone had to offer. And I never saw Lerner pay for any of it. The idea that goods and services cost money fades quickly in the billionaire's world.

If anything required payment, Terry handled it invisibly. She carried stacks of cash and a small photo album filled with charge cards, but her advance people usually dealt with the bill before we even arrived. I told myself not to get used to it, but in a matter of days, I got very used to it.

———

That visit to the San Joaquin Valley brought us to Halloran Family Farms. The old man himself was signing the papers and accepting Lerner's check for $1,500,000. That's a tidy profit on a swamp.

We met on the southern porch of Halloran's Spanish-style estate house, surrounded by almond groves.

Walker Halloran was ninety-six years old and he looked like an unwrapped mummy. He could still walk, sort of. You heard his knees pop on every step. His nurse, Margaret, always stayed within a few feet of him. She never spoke.

Once we were all settled at the patio table in our padded wicker chairs, the old man had to have his say before he signed over the land. He punctuated his points by drumming on the files in front of him with his gaunt yellow fingers.

"Mr. Lerner," he said, "I hope you know what you're doing." Two short breaths preceded each sentence. "You be sure and hire the best thinkers for this idea of yours. Thing is, you won't find anyone who knows more about this land than me. So, listen."

He took a little time to gather his thoughts and pull a cigarette out of a silver case. His shaky fingers brought it to his lips, and the nurse lit it for him with a snap of her lighter. "Thank you, dear," he said.

After a good, deep draw, he continued. "This land is rotten. I learned the hard way. Couldn't grow a thing. Even lost some men."

After another long puff, he continued. "Those bogs have been there as long as the world's been breathing. With each breath the world takes, the bog pulls things in, just a bit. It pulls everything deeper, by barely a measure. The bog moves at the world's pace, not ours, and that's mighty slow."

He opened the files, scrutinizing the aerial photos of the parcel. The two fingers holding his cigarette traced the features of the landscape. "Some things have been down there a long time, and they're better left down there. Have those thinkers of yours study long and move slow. Move careful. Ponder at the world's pace before you go stirring up that bog.

"And whatever you do, leave this stand of willows alone." Halloran thumped a large, green blob in the photo. "These willows, they've been there always, and their roots go all the way down, tangled up with everything that ever was. They're keeping things put. Holding things deep. You leave that stand of willows alone."

His other hand searched through his clothes and around the table until the nurse handed him a pen. "Thank you, dear," he said. "Now, how many damn things do I have to sign?"

———

Six days later, the willows were gone—roots and all. Lerner's crews and heavy gear hauled them up and ground them for compost like they were pulling weeds, a whole acre of them. The trees were on the north side of Central, where they were building a large dock to support the dredging teams, so they had to go.

Our travels calmed down, and I got used to the pulse of the place. I didn't get along with the motorcycles at all, but Emilia rode like Steve McQueen in *The Great Escape*. She'd taken a Kawasaki all over Japan when she covered the Olympics there five years ago, so she had no trouble running circles around everyone on the island, including Lerner.

The dredging machines, each the size of a train engine, were coming via overland transports (courtesy of the Marines) the following week and, in the meantime, the engineers were using a combination of sonar rafts and Nikonos cameras to map the underwater landscape. I spent most of my time with Cyril Matheson, the lead engineer, and his crew.

All Brits. They insisted on keeping good beer in stock. Fine people.

I found Cyril in the courtyard late one morning in the middle of an argument with his soils specialist. A collage of images covered their table. To me, those pictures looked like a bunch of grey smears and hash marks. To the engineers, it was a relief map of everything under the water.

"...and I'm telling you, it can't be tidal," said Matheson.

Steven Andrews, the soils specialist, disagreed. "This entire area is tied to the coastline. Big swells out

in the bay can get the sediment moving around right here. Isn't that why you're sinking all those berms at the estuary's entrance?"

The barn doors on the hangar were open, allowing the nice day to come inside. Even so, most everyone chose to do their work out in the courtyard this morning. I found Emilia eating her toast as she scrutinized pages of proofs. "I was going to give this toast to the ducks," she said, "but they aren't here this morning."

"Maybe they had a meeting," I said. "Sounds like trouble over there."

"Could be," said Emilia. "There's a section where the underwater map keeps changing."

"Is that even possible?"

"It's why they're going round and round." She stacked up the proofs and tucked them into her camera bag. "The grownups are fighting. I'm going to play somewhere else. Maybe get some candid shots of the crew. Want to tag along?"

"No thanks, the story is here today. Seen Lerner?"

"He's with Terry and Ian in the hangar. They're on Terry's walkie if you need them."

"Thanks. I'm going to pretend to work while I eavesdrop." I dropped my pad on the table and took Emilia's place as she headed out.

Matheson rubbed his temples. "I don't know what to think. If the imaging is accurate, this mass of sediment has moved both across the tide and *against it*. There's something pushing things around, maybe some kind of pressure pocket. I don't want a dredger breaking it open."

———

At the east end of the Island, Emilia found Doctor Rankin in a camp chair under an umbrella. He had

video gear spread out on a folding table. Jerry, who was supposed to be helping, stared into the water at the island's edge. Earlier in the week, a digging crew piled up enough sand here to create a tiny beach near the pumping station.

"Hey little guy," said Jerry, looking toward the water.

Emilia went to the table and aimed her Pentax. "Don't look up, Doctor Rankin. Pretend I'm not here," she said, snapping five images. Winding the camera, she tried to focus on Jerry, but she couldn't find a shot. "What's Jerry's deal?"

Rankin checked the reels on a tape machine, wired to a nearby generator, "Mr. Thompson is swooning over an example of the local wildlife, rather than hooking up that receiver."

"I'm not swooning," said Jerry. "I just want to know what this little guy is. I can't tell, and when I get close, he zips down deep. Ah, see. Gone again."

"Good," said Rankin, "then you can return to your work. Miss Berrington, this may interest you. I'm hoping to record a video signal from a camera under the sonar raft. They should pass here soon and when in the receiver's range, these reels will capture the feed."

Emilia's eyes went wide. "Wireless video? Terrific!"

"If it works," said Jerry, cabling up the receiver. "We tried it by Dock Four, but we were too close to the radio tower, too much interference. Hopefully, we'll do better here."

"Maybe your animal friend can help," said Emilia.

"Yeah! I think it's a beaver."

"Not a beaver," said Rankin. "Not here. They are further inland where the water's better."

"Beaver, no doubt," said Jerry. "I'll go ten bucks."

Rankin decided to make this a teaching moment. "It is most likely a raccoon living off our trash. They love the water. I will take your ten dollars."

"Maybe it's a skunk," said Emilia. "Jerry, get *real* close and see."

"If the creature won't let you near it," said Rankin, "how are we going to settle this?"

"Easy," said Thompson. "This rig will get a picture of the thing, which will be a beaver, and I'll get ten bucks."

———

Across the island, at the dock by the radio tower, Matheson and three of his people boarded the sonar raft and set out for the east side. He was a little annoyed they had to do this camera test for Rankin. He wanted to start sounding and solve the mystery of the shifting sediment.

They could use the raft's motor for now but would need to switch to oars for the test. Rankin thought the engine vibration might hinder his camera.

The raft moved quickly, and it only took a few minutes for Rankin and Jerry to come into view. Matheson killed the motor and raised his walkie talkie over his head. Rankin did the same.

"Hello Doc," said Matheson. "We've got your camera rig all hooked up. Meg's on the switch, ready for your orders. Over."

"Excellent," said Rankin. "I think we're ready here, but we have to turn these walkie talkies off. Too much interference. Mr. Thompson will signal you. Can you see him? Over."

Matheson looked toward the shore. Jerry waved

and did terrible jumping jacks. "Yes, I think so," said Matheson. "Signing off." He cut the power to his walkie talkie.

Rankin switched off and powered up the television monitor. He made a few adjustments, but only saw static. "Jerry, tap the yellow wire on the receiver." Jerry obeyed, and the static became a banded image.

"This is so cool," said Emilia.

"Not yet, but we are ever hopeful," said Rankin. "Jerry, have them run the camera."

Jerry cupped his hands in front of his mouth and called to the raft. "Okay, hit the button!"

Meg switched the camera on, and the red light next to the toggle glowed obediently. "It's on!" she hollered.

Rankin's monitor snapped in and out of picture. "Jerry, tell them to come closer to shore." Jerry echoed the request, and the raft rowed in their direction. With an audible pop, the image on the monitor stabilized, and the doctor raised his hand. "There, hold it."

Jerry yelled again and the raft stopped. Rankin hit another switch and the tape reels started turning. Proudly, he pointed at the monitor. "That, Miss Berrington, is the pond, and this is the bottom of the raft."

"It works," said Emilia. She called to Jerry. "You did good, kid, it works."

Jerry faced the raft and extended two thumbs-up, shouting "success!" The crew on the raft cheered.

Rankin's face soured, staring at the monitor. "What is this?"

Emilia looked, but the screen had gone dark. Rankin snatched the tape reels in one hand and his walkie in the other. "We've got to move. Jerry, get away from the water!" He waved his walkie at Matheson.

"What's going on?" asked Emilia.

Matheson saw the panic on the shore and reached for his walkie talkie. Then, half a dozen monsters, each the size of your forearm, leapt into the raft. Two of them clung to Matheson, forcing him into the water. The rest of his crew fell to the floor of the vessel as eight more of the beasts jumped in. Blood sprayed in all directions. Meg managed to stand, screaming, with four of the things tearing her apart. She fell into the pond and the water roiled, like dough being kneaded. A red patch spread.

Jerry looked back at Rankin. "Doc, what is it? We gotta help them." The roll in the water moved from the raft toward shore.

Emilia took a few steps toward Jerry. "Just run! They're coming this way!" He darted past her as she finished the sentence.

"Okay! Gonna get help!" said Jerry.

Rankin pulled Emilia in front of him. "Hangar. Now!" They both ran, trying to catch up to Jerry.

Three of the creatures hobbled up the shoreline and shook themselves dry. As soon as those first few were clear of the water, twenty more of them crawled up.

When Jerry reached the courtyard, he saw people working everywhere. In a blind panic, he yelled about blood and monsters. Rankin and Emilia came close behind, urging everyone to move to the hangar.

The creatures had an irregular gait, but they moved quickly, covering a lot of ground. The pack stayed tight, with the faster ones hopping over the others to move ahead. The whole mass of them tumbled along, falling over each other. A fleshy, chittering avalanche of monsters.

They reached the courtyard and hit seven people at once. Each of them collapsed shrieking.

The rest of the people ran in all directions. I worked with Rankin, trying to get traffic moving towards the hangar, though I didn't know what was going on.

I nearly knocked over Dolores Carn, the medic. "What the hell is this?" she asked.

"Not sure, some kind of attack. We need to get everyone to the hangar."

"Right," she said, grabbing two people by their sleeves. "You and you, come in here and help haul these things to the hanger, now!"

I heard a more familiar voice shouting, "go, go, go!" It was Emilia, directing traffic, facing the beasts, and clicking off a whole roll of film. I told her we had to move. Photos could wait.

She said we'd need the pictures. She was right.

————

Later, Emilia's images provided our first clear look at what would be called the "bog fiends." Many of the creatures in her shots were blurry because they were running. You could only make out their stubby, cylindrical bodies and squat little legs. You might mistake them for pug dogs. But here and there, they were sharp, in focus. It made you sick.

They didn't have a face. There were no eyes. A mass of quivering tendrils occupied the area where a face should have been, like handfuls of nightcrawlers from the bait shop. The top of the head supported a big, boney trapdoor jaw.

They didn't use that jaw to bite. It—scraped. Their tangled worm-face grabbed your arm or your leg. They didn't let go. Then the jaw unhinged and raked, flaying until they reached bare bone. If one got hold of you, more piled on.

But I'm getting ahead of myself.

———

During that first attack, with all the running around, I remember hearing a motorcycle. It was Perkins, one of Matheson's men. He tried to make it to the pontoon bridge, thought he could outrun the things. He didn't even get out of second gear before one of the beasts grabbed hold. Those jaws were savaging his ankle as he accelerated, out of control, right into the radio tower. The bike laid down and the rear tire, still driven by the motor, tangled up the support cables.

The fiends ripped while Perkins hollered. The cables snapped, the metal shrieked, and the tower fell. That din summoned the creatures. The whole pack charged toward the wreckage, creating an opening.

"Get to the hangar, now!" I shouted. Timing or blind luck made my voice heard. Everyone who wasn't already headed there made for the hangar. But one of the creatures heard me, too. It changed course, coming right at me. I spun Emilia around by her arm and we sprinted.

Bart stood in the opening, shepherding people into the hangar as Angela and Gerald rolled the barn doors closer together. He looked right at us. "Keep running, you're the last ones," he shouted, raising his pistol. Emilia ran through to safety. I still had about ten yards to go.

Bart fired, and it looked like he was shooting at me. Then the pain hit. Tendrils had latched onto the back of my thigh.

I dropped.

The jaw grated through my jeans, pulling at my skin. Pieces of my leg tore free. Bart stepped out, put

his pistol right against the damned thing and fired five rounds, killing it.

He dragged me into the hangar. Against everyone's protests, Rankin darted out and grabbed the dead creature. He brought it inside, and the door slammed tight.

The sound of Bart's gun had summoned the pack of monsters. Inside the hangar, everybody shouted at each other. Outside the hangar, the beasts kept throwing themselves against the aluminum walls. Someone I never met before held a pressure bandage on my leg. He said his name was Garth, and that I should "hang in there."

Terry used a bullhorn to call for quiet, and she got it. Dolores did her best to triage the wounded. I heard Lerner's voice, but I couldn't make out the words over the sound of the monsters pounding on the doors. Then, all I saw was Emilia standing over me.

I'd never seen her cry before. "Tony, there you are. What were those things? Did you see them? Oh, God...look at your leg! Garth, hold that thing tighter. We need some help over here! Tony, stay with me!"

I didn't stay with her. Everything went black.

———

There were no dreams. No awareness of the passing of time. I thought I'd simply closed my eyes for a minute.

I'd been out for two hours. The sun would set soon. They had me on a cot under the "Maintenance" banner in the hangar. Nearby there were four other wounded people. The dull ache from my fiercely bandaged right leg brought clear memories of the earlier attack.

The model of the city had been pushed out of the way to make room for everyone to gather around a television.

Rankin gave a presentation. He spoke in hushed tones.

Garth sat next to me. He held a finger to his lips and whispered. "You're awake, good. I'll tell Dolores. Keep quiet. We're pretty sure they react to sound." He walked away, and I heard Lerner's voice.

"Run it again, please," said Lerner.

Rankin rolled his tape back and pushed the "play" button. The television showed the video from the camera under the raft earlier. At first, only the bottom of the vessel and a few plants were visible. Then, about a dozen of those things swam into view. Rankin narrated.

"I've only got thirteen seconds of this. As you can see here, clumsy as they are on land, under the water they move like missiles. Those fireplug bodies are all muscle, and their feet are webbed. They work like paddles. The creatures spin, corkscrewing their way along, fast. Look how this one turns on a dime, then breaches. And this is the one that hits the camera, which ends the recording."

Lerner thanked the doctor and called for Jerry's report. Earlier, when I blacked out, all was chaos. Now, two hours later, everyone's on point. Jerry took a position by the television set. He held a series of drawings, courtesy of Ian Dorney, to help explain his findings. His awkward demeanor had vanished.

"Hello. I've finished the dissection of the creature, learned a lot."

"Have you learned how to kill them?' asked Terry.

"Well, this one died because it got shot five times, twice through the heart. Their heart is in the very

center of their bodies, and the creatures are all muscle. The other bullets didn't get deep. I don't think a pistol is a reliable way to kill one, plus the sound of gunshots will just attract more of them." The room didn't like this information, Lerner signaled for quiet.

"Let him finish," he said.

"Okay," said Jerry. "If you want to slow them down, you can hit the tendrils, this mass of feelers in front. They carry tons of nerves; it won't kill it, but it should stop it for a moment or two. Useful if there's only a few of them, but not for a whole horde.

"They have a regular set of internal organs, plus an extra bladder. I think it helps them swim. Nervous system, circulation, their biology isn't so unusual.

"The feelers in the front are covered in tiny, barbed spines. It's how they hold on. The jaw, up top, looks like it's designed to grab things off the surface of the water. There were duck feathers in the digestive tract. Oh, this may be helpful—the jaw has no teeth. No serrations on the edge. It's made to work like an axe or a hatchet. It rakes and chops."

Chef LaPierre was on edge. "How does that help?"

"It means thick cloth or leather gives some protection. Ricci had a big leather jacket. He managed to take it off and run before they cut through it."

"Pretty bruised up," said Gerald Ricci, rubbing his arm, "but I'll call it a win."

Jerry continued. "And Tony Rodgers had heavy jeans, not those linen shorts everyone likes to wear. He still needed all those stitches, but it could have been...oh, hello Tony." The room shifted focus to me, just as Dolores arrived to check my blood pressure.

"Yes, we're all happy he's awake. Now leave him alone," Dolores said. "You keep going, Jerry." Checking my pressure and pulse, she whispered in

my ear. "It's a big laceration on your leg, Tony. I stitched it up and gave you something for the pain. It's new, Lerner Medical makes it, won't make you stupid." She stopped long enough to note my readings. "Your pulse and pressure are fine, but you can't walk. Don't try. Those terrible things went back to the water an hour ago, got tired of banging on the walls, I suppose. I'll be back with you a little later."

As she stepped away, I shifted on the cot to get a better view of the meeting. Lerner drew on a chalkboard, using lines to join sentences. I couldn't make out the words, but there were a lot of them.

Andrews, the soils specialist, raised his hand. "We still aren't close to an answer on the main question: Where did they come from? I've been here for weeks, working every inch of this place, and never saw a hint of them."

"So, what's different?" asked Lerner. "If these are something new, what's changed? What else is new?"

He got interrupted by a voice, louder than anything I'd heard since waking. It called from the courtyard outside.

"Hello? Where is everybody?" A male voice, young.

Each of the twenty-six heads in the room swung around to the hangar doors. Even mine, and that hurt like hell. The voice called again. "What is this, some kind of gag?" Bart signaled to his people, Angela and Gerald Ricci. They followed him to the windows up front.

"It's David Keith, the kitchen assistant," said Bart. He kept his voice down, but I still heard the urgency.

"No, oh no," said Chef LaPierre. "The Keith brothers, David and Roland, they aren't supposed to be back until tomorrow. They had two days off, went to San Diego."

David's brother, Roland, joined the shouting outside. "David! Can you come back to the boat and help me with this stuff?" The sound came from Dock Four, out of our view.

"Hang on! Just stay there a minute!" David spotted Bart in the window and jogged toward the hangar. Bart kept waving at him, motioning for silence, but he wasn't getting through.

David called out again. "It looks like everybody's in the hangar, and the radio tower is wrecked. Something's weird!" He arrived at the hangar door. "Hey, why are..."

Bart unlocked the door, swung it open and closed, then locked it again. Somehow, he tossed David into the hangar during that move.

"Jeez, Bart, what gives?"

Lerner grabbed him by both shoulders. "David! Is there a walkie in your boat?"

"Yeah, of course."

"What channel?"

Angela had moved to one of the side windows. "Roland isn't by the boat," she said. "He's on the bridge."

She watched Roland Keith walk on the long pontoon bridge leading from Dock Four to the island. "David?" he yelled. "I can't hear you. What are you saying?"

Without making a sound, Angela Jones ducked out the hangar's side door and quickly covered the twenty yards to the spot where the island met the bridge. Bart and Gerald took positions at the door.

She waved at Roland with one hand, using the other to raise a finger to her lips.

Roland saw her and smiled, but once he registered her stance, the smile dropped. He understood. He was in danger.

She motioned for him to come forward. He started to run, so she held up a palm, stopping him. He inhaled to ask a question, but she shook her head with her finger locked to her lips. She repeated her signals, and he took a single, quiet step. Then another.

It took twenty-three steps to get him off the bridge. As soon as he got close enough, Angela covered his mouth and whispered in his ear.

"See your brother?" David waved from the window next to the hangar's side door. "He's safe. You'll be safe if you listen and do as I say. I'm going to count to three. On three, run as fast as you can through the door, where Bart is. Do you understand?" The setting sun provided enough light for Angela to see the terror in his eyes as he nodded.

A small splash came from the water's edge behind them. Two of the fiends had hopped onto the island. Every few seconds, they snapped their heads in a new direction with their tendrils stretched all the way out.

They were seeking.

Roland's eyes went even wider. Angela forced him to look at her. She demanded silence, took her hand off his mouth, and drew her pistol.

The fiends were moving along the edge, toward the bridge. She raised her free hand in a fist. She mouthed "one," swinging out one finger. Then "two," with two fingers.

On "three," Roland sprinted for the door, feet pounding with each stride. The pair of fiends turned toward him and charged. Angela spun around to them and emptied her pistol. She hit each one in the tendrils, stopping them, but the sound of gunshots had summoned more.

Roland made it through the door and Bart reached out his hand for Angela. She got within five steps of

him when the beasts caught up to her. She called to Bart.

"Close the doors, keep them safe!" Then she fell under ten of the monsters.

Everyone moved away from the windows and walked slowly to the center of the room. Bart pulled the door shut. Roland and David held each other tight, asking what was happening.

—

The Keith brothers had run out of money and decided to come back a day early. They parked their jeep at City Limits (where I first met Lerner) and took a launch from there, just like they were supposed to. A cluster of swamp grass got tangled up in their outboard, killing the motor, and that's what saved them.

They had to row, quietly, the rest of the way. The fiends must have been on the other side of Central when the Keiths started making noise. No one else was due to the island until the following day, when some Marines were arriving to go over plans for the dredger transport. Without the radio, we couldn't warn them.

"Can't we do the same thing the other way?" asked Terry. "I mean, take quiet steps across the bridge, row the launch to City Limits, then take one of the Jeeps and get help?"

Bart aimed his flashlight out the side window. "Not right now. There's six of them by the edge and even more on the bridge."

Emilia joined him and put her hand on his shoulder. "Should you even be looking out there?" It had only been half an hour since Angela fell.

Bart shifted the flashlight. "Look, over there," he

said. Reluctantly, Emilia peered out the window. There were no signs of the earlier attack. "It's like it never happened," said Bart. "They took everything, everything she was. She looked right at me and told me to keep you all safe, so that's what I'm doing. They can't take that."

Emilia put her head on his shoulder. They stood there together for what seemed a long time.

At the chalkboard, Lerner adjusted his lists. "We know loud noises attract them. We know a shot to the feelers will hurt them. We still don't know where they came from."

I had been sorting through all of Emilia's proof sheets and pictures. "The willows," I said. "It's what changed, what's new. An acre of willow trees got hauled away. The old man, the almond guy. He said something about them."

Terry flipped through her notes. "Walker Halloran. He said they were holding things back. He said to leave the willows alone."

Gerald Ricci, the security officer, shook his head. "You mean, these things were bottled up in the bog, and those trees were the cork? That sounds crazy."

"I'll tell you what sounds crazy," said Lerner, "fifteen people killed by monsters, by some kind of—bog fiends. *That* sounds crazy, but it really happened, so let's not call anything 'crazy.' If they *were* under the willows, how did they get there?"

Rankin and Jerry, who had continued studying the dead fiend, joined the group. "They've always been there, near as we can figure," said Rankin, cleaning his glasses. "We've been pouring through our zoology texts, and we have a theory."

"Let's hear it," said Lerner.

"This is going to sound odd," said Rankin. "We think they are moles."

"Aye. Moles from hell who want to eat your face," said Dorney.

"Well, they *became* moles," said Jerry. "All life started in the water, and these are the mole's aquatic ancestors."

"They are prehistoric, savage," said Rankin. "Several species probably branched out from this version, some evolving into the common garden moles you're familiar with."

"You may have seen a star-nosed mole," said Jerry. "They live up north. They have a version of that feeler mass at the front. Another branch may have evolved the protruding jaw into a bill, becoming the platypus."

"This explanation fits our events," said Rankin. "A creature from the distant past, unnoticed or newly awakened. Like the tahake bird or coelacanth."

Terry stood up, pointing at her notes. "It happened to him. To Halloran, he said some of his people died." She showed the pages to Rankin, then Lerner. "He said the land was rotten. He said he lost people, and whatever you do, leave those willow trees alone."

"He tried to grow rice, way back in the thirties," said Lerner. "He must have cleared some of those trees to make way for the paddies. Those things killed his men, and he closed down the operation."

"But this isn't magic," said Andrews. "Those aren't haunted trees, and this isn't a curse. Prehistoric or not, they're still animals. The doc said so. There's something about this animal and those trees, a scientific connection of some kind." He rubbed his neck. "It's giving me a headache. Is there aspirin?"

"Case of it, right over there," said Dolores.

Jerry lit up. He ran to the case and grabbed a bottle. "The willows! Doc, come on. Andrews is right.

There's a connection, and I think it's chemical!" Both returned to the dissection table.

Everyone gathered around the table until they saw the creature's remains, then most of them did a sharp turn and went back to the main area of the hangar. Jerry gloved up and started forcing aspirin into different parts of the creature.

"I don't know what you expect to see," said Rankin.

"Not certain...constriction of the tissues, some kind of nerve occlusion, autonomic muscle response."

Terry stood between them. "Why?"

"The aspirin, it's primarily acetylsalicylic acid," said Jerry. "It's a concentration of salicylic acid, which is the form you find in nature. It's in plants, specifically in Spiraeas—like willows. They're loaded with the stuff. The Egyptians used willow bark to relieve pain, but it wasn't magic. It was the salicylic acids reducing inflammation, for real."

"Of course," said Rankin, "Salicylic acid in its pure state is used as a preservative, and it also works on the nervous system, circulation, and digestion. A biological reaction along with the deep bog could hold a group of these—what did Malcolm call them? Bog fiends? Yes, it could hold these bog fiends in stasis for any number of centuries."

"I'm not following," said Lerner.

"Picture a substantial horde of these creatures attacking some large animal stuck in the bog, right at the center of the willow grove," said Rankin, "but instead of getting an easy meal, they get stuck in the bog themselves. Hundreds of them. Where other creatures sank into the bog and died, this particular species reacted to the salicylic acid that had been leaching from the willows for ages. Vulnerable to it.

They had a cataleptic reaction. They stopped moving, barely a heartbeat."

"So, the combination of this animal, the bog, and the salicylic acid preserved them, like suspended animation," said Terry.

"Exactly," said Rankin. "Once the willows were gone, and the creatures drawn up with the roots, well, after a few days free of the salicylic acid's effects, they started moving again."

"That would explain our shifting sediments," said Andrews.

"Yes. And today," said Jerry, "they've become active. Fully animated."

"So, what does all this mean?" asked Lerner.

"It means a concentrated dose of salicylic acid might paralyze them, put them under again—instantly," said Jerry. "But this specimen is dead, so there's no circulation, no nerve transmission. These tissues aren't reacting at all."

"Those tissues are reacting with my nose," said Dorney. "And it's making me sick."

"Yes, the odor is strong," said Rankin. "The bile sack ruptured and evacuated a digestive sludge."

"You aren't helping," said Dorney, holding a tissue to his face.

"I know what *can* help," said Jerry. "We need to test a living specimen."

"What are you going to do," said Dorney, "smack it with a willow branch?"

"No. First, I'm going to grind all this aspirin into a powder. Then I'm going to dust the bog fiends with it. And if I'm right, the little bastards will drop like rocks."

———

The aspirin came from Lerner Medical in bulk packaging. Big bottles with three thousand pills in each. It sounds like a lot, but once it got ground up into a powder, it only filled a one-gallon bucket.

But we still didn't know if the powder could stop the creatures. And we didn't have enough of the stuff to run a whole series of tests. Instead, we put everything we had on our best plan, then we split the powder supply.

One third for a test, the rest for execution.

It might be enough to keep someone safe while they followed Terry's plan: Move down the bridge to Dock Four, row a launch from there to City Limits, then take a jeep to get help.

Silence was our primary defense—taking quiet, careful steps to keep the bog fiends from coming in the first place. If that failed, the powder might work as a secondary defense, to quietly disable them. But first, we had to know for certain if the powder stopped them, and the quantity needed to do so. And that part of the plan fell to Bart Charles.

———

Half an hour later, near midnight, Bart stood in full motorcycle leathers at the shoreline on the east side of Central. There, Rankin's tattered umbrella marked the spot where the bog fiends first climbed out of the water. The sonar raft had drifted to the opposite bank. He saw it in the moonlight.

This test had to happen far from the hangar in case it failed. Bart had a box of ground aspirin tucked under his left arm and a flashlight in his right hand. His pistol, a last resort, was holstered. If he fired it, he might as well ring the dinner bell.

He had followed a circuit between buildings that

kept him out of the courtyard and away from the water. So far, he hadn't encountered any fiends.

His eyes closed for a moment, and he cleared his mind, remembering each thing he had to do to make this worthwhile. Then he crept near the water's edge.

The crickets and frogs were silent. The soft hum of the pumping station was the only sound he heard. Kneeling, he aimed the flashlight beam low, so the light broke through the water.

There were four of the beasts just below the surface, facing the pumping station. He moved the light and saw no reaction. He stood. No reaction. He backed up ten feet from the water.

There, he shook some of the powder out of the box, forming a tiny berm parallel to the bank. If the fiends came up, they'd have to cross it. Ten feet back from there, he laid down a second berm, thicker than the first. He felt like he was marking out a softball field with chalk.

With light steps, he moved back another ten feet. There, he used the rest of the powder to make a third berm, thicker than the other two. He pulled a walkie talkie from his belt and propped it up in the dirt behind the last berm.

With his head on a swivel, he moved to a space behind the generators. He had a clear view from there. He pulled a second walkie out of this belt, trying to stop his hands from shaking. He rested his right thumb on the button marked "call," and aimed the flashlight at the water.

He pressed the button.

The red light pulsed on the other walkie, and the tone it made echoed across the marsh. He kept the button engaged; the tone didn't stop. *"Come on, get it, come on!"* he thought.

And they came. All four of the bog fiends moved

up the shore and made for the source of the noise. They crossed the first line without a pause, and Bart's heart sank. As they crossed the second line, each of them jerked and rolled over stiff. Bart released the button on the walkie. Once again, the hum from the pumping station became the only sound.

He waited to see if they shook off the effects, or if more of them showed up. After what he supposed felt like enough time, he pulled a canvas duffel bag off his back and approached the motionless creatures.

Their tendrils had curled up into a flat, honeycombed pad. The jaws were shut tight, and the legs were tucked against the bodies. He pushed one with his foot. It rolled over like a plastic toy. No twitches, no breath.

Flinching, he lifted a bog fiend into the duffle. The handles would have to keep it closed; he didn't want to risk the noisy zipper. Turning to head back to the hangar, he stepped over the third line of powder. It was untouched.

It was also too valuable to leave behind.

He used his hands to scoop the powder back into the box, being careful not to get dirt into it, keeping one eye on the motionless bog fiends just a few feet away. Try as he might, he couldn't look at them without seeing Angela's fall.

Rage filled his chest. Clouding his reason. After he put the last handful of powder in the box, he stood, took three long steps, and kicked one fiend. It went end over end like a football, splashing twenty yards out in the pond. Satisfied, he gathered up the duffle, so the handles and flashlight shared one hand.

As he knelt for the box, he saw a bog fiend coming down the path from the courtyard. It swept back and forth, moving in a search pattern with its tendrils outstretched. He didn't see a way to avoid it.

Bart stood up slowly, still gripping the duffle and flashlight. With his foot, he tipped the box over. It made a small *"ploff"* sound as the powder fell out. He used the tip of his boot to form it into a rough line, then he whistled.

The creature bolted at him, crossed the line, and dropped like a rock. Immediately, Bart glided through the gap between the generators. He had to get back on track.

He padded along the same route he used earlier. It was still clear. As he moved around the trash cans behind the guard shack, the hangar came into view. The barn doors in front made too much noise, so Ricci waited for him at the side entry.

A small growl came from the cans. Bart turned and found a raccoon in front of them.

It shifted into a defensive stance. Bart stood still, hoping not to aggravate it. The growl got louder, so Bart backed away one step. The raccoon didn't like that either, so it ran off, knocking the lid off one of the cans as it scrambled away. The lid not only crashed when it fell, it rolled around and made more noise as it settled.

Three bog fiends appeared.

Determined, Bart moved toward the hangar door, still trying to stay silent. Two of the fiends went after the raccoon. The remaining fiend struck Bart's leg, just above the ankle. The jaw scraped, raking at the leathers, but Bart refused to scream. He kept pushing toward the door, where he knew Ricci waited.

He hopped, dragging one leg behind, until he got close enough for Ricci to get him inside. As the door shut behind him, Bart finally screamed, "Get it off! Get it off!"

"Drop down, flat on your belly!" It was Dorney, holding a shovel over his shoulder like a three-wood.

Bart went down and Dorney nailed the beast with a drive that put Jack Nicklaus to shame. The thing bounced off the wall, leaving a brown stain. In seconds, it got up again, clearly injured but scrambling right back at Dorney.

Terry appeared with a pipe and destroyed its head. She used the pipe to nudge it a few times. "This one's finished," she said. "Bart, are you okay?"

He tried his best to speak. "The second line stopped them...the one-inch line...and there's no reaction to light," then he passed out. He still held the duffle bag. The back of his right calf had been hollowed out.

———

Dolores stopped the bleeding and got Bart stable. She was certain he'd lose that leg, but he risked losing much more if he didn't get to a hospital in the next twelve hours.

Rankin and Jerry examined the stunned bog fiend. Everyone worried it might wake and attack them. Chef LaPierre made things safer by trussing the creature up securely with twine. Dorney said it looked like "Thanksgiving on Mars."

The examination proved the fiend was alive, but with the faintest heartbeat and almost no other vital signs. It had no reaction to heat, punctures, sharp blows, or loud noises. Even when they washed away the residual powder, it remained in stasis.

After all their testing, they packed its "face" with more powder, just to be sure, and zipped it up in the duffle. Gerald Ricci, the best rower, would be taking the horrid thing with him to a jeep, parked at City Limits.

The group had made a packet containing Doctor

Rankin's videotape, some of Emilia's pictures, and a brief on the situation written by yours truly. That brief got typed up at inhuman speed by Garth Trent, Terry's travel coordinator. The packet got tucked into Ricci's shirt as he pulled on a set of leathers.

He'd get to a phone and dial a special number we had for the Marines at Camp Pendleton. Lerner's weapons contracts gave him access. Ricci would read them the brief and if it wasn't enough for them, he'd spend another hour and drive to the base. There, he'd hand over everything we had, including the bog fiend in the duffle bag. Hopefully, it would be enough to get a rescue mission running.

Terry took him aside and handed him a card.

"If there's any fuss about cost," she said, "just give them this."

"A Banker's Trust Card? I've already got one in my wallet. How does this help?"

She shook her head. "This is an *Iridium* Banker's Trust Card, the only one they've ever issued. It solves problems. Even military problems."

"Okay."

"Lerner Medical has a warehouse in Santa Ana. I bet they've got aspirin by the ton. They may even have the raw material in powder form. Oh, and Malcolm has wineries in Escondido with their own planes and pilots for crop dusting. They're close if you need them."

"Okay."

"If Major Pike is in the room, he's going to want to come in with flamethrowers and machine guns. You need to make them understand these things are hard to kill with bullets, and the salicylic acid has kept them in check for centuries. It's our best bet to put them down again."

"Terry," said Lerner.

"Should I be writing this down? Let me write this down," said Terry, looking for her notes.

"Terry," said Lerner, "You know I have to go with him. It's the only way they'll listen." She looked at him with those rare eyes of hers. They moved back and forth, looking for an idea that kept Lerner safe in the hangar while getting help here as quickly as possible.

Such an idea didn't exist. Lerner had to go. Terry threw her arms around him and begged him not to get creative, to stick to the plan. He promised and moved across the room to get his leathers.

"Hey Emilia," said Lerner, "can you get a picture of me and Gerald, all suited up and ready? Might be important."

Emilia sat next to Bart, telling him stories and holding his hand while he slept. "The camera's right there," she said. "Terry can do it. Just point and click."

She never let anyone touch her gear before.

———

At 1:30 am, Gerald Ricci and Malcom Lerner quietly closed the hangar's side door behind them and took careful steps toward the pontoon bridge. Lerner carried the duffle and a flashlight. Ricci had a bucket containing the rest of our ground aspirin and a large scoop to spread it around.

There were no fiends by the door, but there were three at the bridge. Ricci got close, without alerting them, and scooped out a line of powder. He whistled one time, and they charged. Everyone at the windows flinched as the bog fiends crossed the powder line but relaxed a little when they saw them fall over. Ricci poked one with his boot and shared a nod with

Lerner, who gave the high sign to the crowd at the windows.

Crossing the pontoon bridge came next. They put powder lines down in a staggered pattern and kept their steps light and careful. At one point, they heard splashing about 5 yards behind them. Lerner's flashlight revealed one creature hopping onto the bridge. It shook itself dry, hit the powder, then went stiff and rolled back into the water. Both men had to work to stifle their laughter.

From the hangar, only half the bridge was visible. Soon, they were out of our view. We didn't risk using the walkies. Feedback or static happened too frequently. We just had to wait.

No one talked much.

———

The dawn light came through the shade film on the windows, turning the room blue. Doctor Rankin spoke. "Is anyone awake?"

Everyone was awake.

"We should have another plan ready," he said. "In case..."

"They need time," said Terry.

"Yes, I understand," said Rankin. "And it is my great hope they will be successful. But we should have our next steps ready in case they are not."

I'd been thinking the same thing, though I didn't want to. Lerner and Ricci may have been killed before they reached the boat, and we'd have no way of knowing.

"Whatever this plan is, it has to end with all of us getting off Central," said Steven Andrews. "City Limits is close, but we might consider heading toward the estuary and out toward the coast."

"There's a couple of big launches at Dock 6," said Jerry. "Another at Dock 9. Those three are enough to fit everyone, but we'd have to carry Bart. Carry everyone who can't walk."

It got quiet again.

———

As the hours passed, the morning sun ignored the shade film and filled the room. Any other time, I would have said it was a nice day out.

"Sorry Tony," said Dolores Carn. She had just finished changing the dressing on my leg, and it hurt like hell. "I'm doing what I can."

"Understood," I said.

"Thought I'd never have to do front-line medical again," she said. "Hell, I'm retired from the service." Her voice shifted to a whisper. "Bart's getting bad. He needs I.V. meds. Proper treatment. Hospital treatment."

Emilia had fallen asleep with her head on Bart's chest.

"Two hours," said Dolores. "We're going to have to make some ugly choices in two more hours."

Terry heard everything. "You're right," she said. "That's when those Marines are supposed to visit about the dredging. They are due at noon."

"So, that's when we'll know," said Dorney. "If the Marines show up for a meeting, our boys failed. If they show up in force, they succeeded. I've been sitting here all morning trying to figure a plan to get us to those launches young Jerry mentioned. Other than a heated sprint, I can't come up with anything."

Andrews nodded. "Same here. Without the aspirin powder, all we can do is outrun them."

"We put a lot of things on the chalkboard last night," I said. "Are any of them sound?"

"Sound!" Jerry Thompson lit up and walked a tight circle, thinking. "Yesterday, on the other side of Central, the raft. We can use the sonar gear!"

"It might work," said Rankin. "But the raft has probably drifted."

"Could you maybe include the rest of us in what you're thinking?" asked Dorney.

Everyone shifted their focus to Jerry. "The sonar raft sends sound waves down through the water," he said. "They bounce off the bottom and back up again, and the equipment uses the data to map what's down there. Mr. Andrews knows more about it than I do."

"You're doing fine. Keep going," said Andrews.

"It's a concentrated sound, and we can aim it," said Jerry. "If the raft is working, it might lead the little bastards away. Like the Pied Piper."

Everyone's sleepless wheels were turning. Jerry's plan made sense.

Almost.

"But Jerry," I said. "Someone has to go across the entire island, find this raft, and then maybe swim out to it, right?"

"Where did you see it last?" asked Andrews.

"East side," said Jerry. "In front of the pumping stations."

"It's very still over there," said Andrews. "The raft won't have moved far. But Tony makes a good point. Unless it's drifted into the sand by the pumping station, someone will need to swim out to it, climb aboard, and start the machinery."

"You are absolutely right," said Rankin. "Fortunately, we have a few hours to figure out how to best ameliorate that risk. And hopefully, last night's endeavor will make this plan superfluous."

"The way you talk, Doctor," said Dorney. "'Ameliorate. Superfluous.' Well, here's a fact for your chalkboard. I'm the best swimmer here. Get me a set of those leathers and there's your plan done."

———

The closer we got to noon, the edgier everyone became. Dorney kept insisting on heading to the raft without delay. As he put it: "If this sonar business gets cocked up, you'll need another plan. Best to know now."

The "now" plan got shot down, repeatedly. Lerner and Ricci were our best option, and we had to wait for them. Not to mention, whoever led the bog fiends away on the raft probably wouldn't return. Plus, Dorney had appointed himself to this mission when there may have been a better candidate.

Still, bickering about this alternate plan did a decent job of filling the time. Dorney was the best swimmer, no question there. But Jerry also swam well, and he had experience with the equipment. The pros and cons of sending one or the other or both were discussed, debated, and diagrammed.

Until we heard engines in the distance. Just before noon.

"Oh no," said Terry. "It's those Marines." She grabbed a walkie. "I've got to see if I can raise them, warn them."

Dolores smiled. "No need, Terry. Lerner and Ricci got through."

She heard the same thing I did, a Chinook helicopter. Nothing else sounds like those twin motors. Everyone shoved their faces against the windows, trying to look up as the helicopter settled into a hover over the swamp past Dock Four.

A voice rang out over their P.A., "Attention in the hangar, please stay inside. Switch on your walkie talkie to channel four. Your United States Marine Corps is running a rescue operation, and it is important you follow instructions and maintain communication. Repeating, stay inside and set your walkie talkie to channel four."

Dolores grabbed the walkie from Terry. "Hangar copies, channel four open per instructions. This is Dolores Carn, Army Medical Corps, Sergeant First Class, retired. We have six wounded, avulsion injuries and severe lacerations. All are stable, for the moment. One unconscious, all non-ambulatory, all in dire need of a hospital,—yesterday. Who am I speaking to? Over."

The walkie talkie hissed, "...um, this is Malcolm Lerner. Hi Dolores, let me turn you over to Major Pike. Over."

Major Pike stepped us through the plan. We were to stay inside and follow instructions. The wounded would be lifted in basket stretchers to the Chinook from the courtyard. The rest were going out the side door to get picked up by a prototype LVTP7 Amphibious Troop Transport.

If a tank and a boat had a huge, ugly baby, it would look like the LVTP7.

Dolores let me lean by a window so I could see. Terry ran in circles, gathering necessities and lining people up by the door.

Emilia asked if anyone could take pictures while she monitored Bart.

"That's a good way to get your camera stolen," said Bart. "Besides, those pictures will be lousy if anyone else takes them." Then he opened his eyes.

"You shouldn't be awake," said Dolores. She trotted over and checked his vitals. They worried her.

Emilia gave him a kiss and said, "all right, I'll take

the pictures, but the first shot is going to be you and Dolores."

"Don't you dare," said Dolores. "I look like crap." She tapped on a syringe and brought it to Bart's arm. "This is more pain medication. You'll feel a pinch."

"I'm pretty punchy, Ma'am. Pinch all you want," said Bart. "Emilia, people are going to need to see this, so you need to get the shots. I'll go tree basket around and around. It will span paper toffee feet." Then he drifted off.

"I thought the new medication didn't make you stupid," I said.

"It's not what I gave him," said Dolores. "He needed the elephant drops."

The Chinook's P.A. echoed across the swamp again. "We are starting the operation. Please stay inside the hangar until instructed to do otherwise. Keep your walkie talkie on channel four."

The copter took a position over the courtyard. The remarkable noise sent the bog fiends into a frenzy. At least twenty of them jumped for the chopper again and again. That number doubled in less than a minute.

The Chinook hovered at roughly fifty feet when the doors on each flank opened. I could just make out the Marines inside as they pitched cotton bags the size of hay bales out of the aircraft. The bags landed in the courtyard with a thump, broke open, and sent a plume of white powder in all directions. Anyone new to the scene would think they were dumping giant sacks of flour, but we knew it was acetylsalicylic acid.

I saw one bag land right on top of a bog fiend, crushing it. "Good shot," said Dolores, "for a Marine."

Those that weren't crushed were dusted heavily, sending them into stasis. The bags kept dropping, cre-

ating knee-high piles of the powder all over the courtyard, and as more of the fiends ran in, driven wild by the buffeting of the Chinook's twin blades, they hit the white dust and curled up tight.

In just five minutes, the Marines had created a rough oval of powder around the perimeter of the courtyard. Then the first squad zip-lined from the craft. They wore full helmets and body armor. Half of them carried shovels, which they used to close gaps in the oval berm surrounding them.

By the mess hall, two bog fiends found their way through a gap and jumped one man. He fell in a spastic roll, making frantic snow angels in the aspirin dust until the things fell off. Then he stood back up and started shoveling again, like it never happened.

The Chinook came around the building and the area between the hangar and the bridge got the same treatment. Of course, this took a lot less powder. A second squad zip-lined down and started shaping the new berms, then the helicopter moved back to its position over the courtyard.

The first squad had completed a path leading to the barn doors. They slid the doors open and carried the injured one at a time, starting with Bart, to a staging area where they were winched in rescue baskets up to the Chinook. It wouldn't be my turn for some time.

Meanwhile, two Marines took positions at the hangar's side door as the LVTP7 jumped over the bank by the pontoon bridge, spun around, then dropped the back hatch right at their feet.

The pair outside turned and signaled us to open the door. They stepped right in and got to work. One of them started sizing people up, so he could put them in the right order for evacuation. He didn't re-

ally have to do anything because Terry had it just right.

The other man took off his helmet. It wasn't a Marine. It was Malcolm Lerner. "I had to make sure this worked," he said. We all cheered.

"We've got a solution here, a *real* solution," he said. "We can fix this."

"What? This is working for the moment," said Terry. "But then what? There's probably more of those things, lots more, further out."

"We can drop that powder by the metric ton—everywhere. Cover the whole site with it. Replant the willow trees."

"Then what?" asked Terry.

"Maybe we can mix it with the concrete for the pilings. Plant even more willows for the landscaping."

"Malcolm..."

"Maybe use it on the pavement. Suspend it in the paint."

"Malcolm!" I had never heard Terry yell. "We can't let people live here. We've always had contingencies for a natural disaster stopping the project. That's what this is. Once we get out, we have to make sure no one ever comes here again."

The models and maps of Primo were piled in a corner of the hangar. Lerner walked to them, reached out, and touched the discarded pieces of a dream he nearly made real.

Then he drew in a deep breath, and let the dream go.

"We've got copies of everything at the main office in San Francisco," he said. "Maybe we can use some of these ideas in Port Mansfield."

It took just over an hour for those troops to get us out of there. The last one to board the LVTP7 was

Malcolm Lerner. The last person to get hauled up into the Chinook was me.

The Marines stayed for another week using machine guns, flamethrowers, and three tons of acetylsalicylic acid to get the situation "under control."

———

You know the rest. The deaths, injuries, and evacuations were blamed on a methane gas pocket. It caused a massive flash fire during our dredging operations. The area remains sealed by state order until further notice. The settlements with the decedents' next of kin were also sealed. Lerner made sure we were all well compensated and received the best counseling. The injured continue to receive the latest, most effective treatments, free of charge.

Each survivor had signed the same weighty nondisclosure contracts I did, assuring our silence. I'm breaking that silence with this piece, but my other contract with *The Globe* requires me to deliver this article about the launch of Primo. I can't do both, so we'll see which contract I'm allowed to breach.

I've interviewed most of the people involved, and none of them hold Lerner to blame. Many donated their extra compensation to charity. Bart spent a lot of his extra compensation on Emilia's engagement ring, and his new leg is like something out of *Star Trek;* he doesn't even need crutches.

Of the six of us who got lacerations in a swamp, I was the only one who developed an infection. Tetanus, very nasty. I've been told I'll be able to bend my knee again in a month.

———

On a regular rotation, you'll see the Coast Guard or the Marines sending small craft into the wetlands of Southern California, sounding their air horns and sinking what looks like concrete pods.

Those pods aren't made of concrete, and they dissolve over time. If you ever have a headache, just dive into any lagoon south of Dana Point. You'll feel better right away. But don't make any loud noises, just to be sure.

Trivia

Bog Fiends had its drive-in theatrical run in the summer of 1970. The movie was serialized in the pulp magazine *Weird Adventure* the following year. Those pages are reprinted here.

This was the last World Cinema Group release on black and white film.

Shot in eight days in and around the Lake O'Neill Recreation Area of Camp Pendleton, California.

The United States Marine Corps agreed to help with the production of the film so long as the USMC "saved the day and were heroes" in the movie. This agreement enabled the production to use actual troops, a Chinook helicopter, amphibious landing craft, and the Camp Pendleton Marine Base.

Edward G. Robinson's scenes as Walker Halloran were shot in a single day. The patio of his Palm Springs home served as Halloran's porch.

Having spent most of his career working on television and feature westerns, director Theodore Barrett didn't want to make a "monster movie." William Sternbaum, who wrote fourteen features for World Cinema Group, reworked his script with Barrett to make it "more like a frontier town under attack by a gang of outlaws." Barrett would go on to direct five more pictures for World Cinema Group, including the infamous paratrooper epic, "Commandos from 30,000 Feet," their only war movie.

Stop motion was considered to realize the bog fiends, but the process was too expensive. The closeups of the tendrils making up the creatures' faces are the only shots where stop motion was used.

For wider shots of the horde of bog fiends, pug dogs in lightweight costumes were used to portray the monsters. Screenwriter William Sternbaum regretted comparing the bog fiends to dogs in his script, as he may have given the producers the idea to use them.

Close ups of the bog fiends attacking their victim's extremities were achieved with puppets tearing up "flesh-colored sacks of liverwurst and chocolate syrup." These scenes were cut from most European versions of the film.

The "aspirin powder" was actually ordinary field chalk, readily available at the time for $.05 per pound.

About the Author

Bret Nelson is an Emmy Award-winning creator. When he's not writing stories, he makes TV shows and games. Over the years, he's worked with Kermit the Frog, Buzz Lightyear, and Conan the Cimmerian.

Right now, he's busy with projects he's not allowed to talk about (that's what the contracts say).